KATE THOMPSON

The *Alchemist's* Apprentice

THE BODLEY HEAD
London

for Jacob

First published in Great Britain by The Bodley Head,
an imprint of Random House Children's Books

This edition published 2002

3 5 7 9 10 8 6 4 2

Papers used by Random House Children's Books are natural,
recyclable products made from wood grown in sustainable forests.
The manufacturing processes conform to the environmental
regulations of the country of origin

The Bodley Head is published by Random House Children's Books,
61-63 Uxbridge Road, London W5 5SA,
a division of The Random House Group Ltd,
in Australia by Random House Australia (Pty) Ltd,
20 Alfred Street, Milsons Point, Sydney, NSW 2061, Australia,
in New Zealand by Random House New Zealand Ltd,
18 Poland Road, Glenfield, Auckland 10, New Zealand,
and in South Africa by Random House (Pty) Ltd,
Endulini, 5A Jubilee Road, Parktown 2193, South Africa

THE RANDOM HOUSE GROUP Limited Reg. No. 954009

ISBN 0 370 32545 1

A CIP catalogue record for this book is available
from the British Library

Designed and typeset in Founder's Caslon and Ornaments
by Douglas Martin
Printed and bound in Great Britain by
Biddles Ltd, Guildford

Chapter One

In the tiny yard behind the forge, the cock crowed. Jack was on his feet before he was awake; before William could get to him and drag him out of bed. He bent beneath the dusty rafters of the loft, pulling himself up from ugly dreams which kept trying to drag him back down among his blankets. He swayed on his feet, then stretched and yawned and opened his eyes. It was still dark, but he didn't need to see to know that William wasn't there.

He remembered now. William had hurt his back shoeing a horse the day before and Tom, the farrier they were both apprenticed to, had sent him home for a few days to recover. It meant that Jack would have one less bully to worry about.

It also meant that there would be twice as much work.

The cock crowed again. From the street outside, Jack heard the first clatter of buckets and the wheezy voice of the pump handle as the neighbourhood's earliest risers began the day. Propping himself against the slope of the roof, he shook the spiders out of his clothes and pulled them on.

Treading carefully to avoid the crunch of cockroaches beneath his bare feet, Jack crossed the rough wooden timbers of the floor and climbed down the ladder into the forge. Tom was always the last to arrive, but Jack had never been in the forge without William there, bossing and boasting. He stopped for a moment, looking into the silent darkness, breathing in the familiar smells of smoke and burnt hooves. It was a rare, peaceful moment, but he couldn't allow it to last for long. There was too much work to be done.

The bolt on the back door was stiff. It grated and dug into Jack's hand, but eventually slid across. In the little yard behind it, the farrier's pony whickered gently, anxious for his breakfast.

Jack laughed. 'Coming, Dobbs,' he said.

The morning was dry and clear. The stars were still shining, though dawn was dimming them fast. Cocks were crowing now from every direction and, as he walked across the dew-damp cobbles, Jack could hear the noises of the town as it woke. From behind the thin doors and shutters of the houses around the forge, people coughed and hawked or called to each other or grumbled. Jack gathered an armful of hay from the shelter in the corner of the yard and stood at the door of the tiny stall where Dobbs spent most of his days. The pony grabbed a mouthful, and Jack stood and rubbed his neck while he ate it. Though Dobbs rarely showed any sign of interest in anything other than food, Jack felt a special affinity with him. They were the underdogs at the forge, the ones who couldn't answer back. Sometimes it seemed that they were both there for no other purpose than to bear the brunt of Tom's bad temper, and William's, too. Yet there was nothing they could do about it. There was nowhere else for either of them to go.

Reluctantly, Jack threw the rest of the hay over the door and returned to the forge. With difficulty he pulled back the heavy bolts and opened up the double doors at the front of the building. Outside them, a little way up the street, a queue had formed at the pump. Jack had known most of the people there all his life and exchanged greetings with them as he bolted the doors open. He knew, however, that despite their friendly acceptance of him, he was seen as a bit of a joke; the puniest apprentice ever taken on by a blacksmith in London.

He went back inside and turned his attention to the fire. Sometimes, when the smith had been busy late into the evening, there were still embers glowing in it, but this morning it was quite cold. Jack raked out the ashes carefully, then gathered tinder and kindling and lit them with a spark from a flint. In the dry, summer conditions they burned fiercely, and Jack had to move quickly, piling up charcoal around them before they burnt out. Then, relieved to have got a good start on the work, he began to sweep the floor.

By the time Tom arrived, yawning and stretching, still bleary-eyed from the previous night's ale, the fire had heated up well and Jack was standing proudly above a heap of dusty nail-ends and hoof-parings. The last of the darkness had been washed from the sky and the queue at the pump had dwindled.

Tom peered into the furnace and nodded approvingly. 'Boost her up, now, lad,' he said. 'Nicholson's cob has to be done first thing, and I still haven't finished that gate for old Martin.'

He began to sort through some pieces of iron leaning against the opposite wall and Jack watched him, fascinated by his strength.

'Jack will grow on.' It was a neighbour, Peg, who had brought him to Tom, after his mother died. 'He just had a bad start, that's all. He'll catch up.'

Tom had stared at him in astonishment, then looked at Peg as though she were out of her mind.

'Someone has to take him,' she had said. 'He has no one now.'

Jack still couldn't understand why he had been accepted. If Tom had pity in his heart it was buried very deep beneath his drunkenness and ill humour. He could only assume that Peg, who had been his mother's best friend, had some mysterious influence over Tom or had called upon some favour that was owed. Because as he watched the blacksmith's broad shoulders and muscular arms, Jack knew that what she had said was not true. He would never grow into anything like Tom. His legs were bowed with rickets and his narrow ribcage showed clearly through his skin, above a belly that seemed always to be empty. Beside the bulk of the blacksmith he felt like a puppet or a rag doll, with bony shoulders and tiny, skinny arms. As a blacksmith's apprentice he was a dead loss and he knew it. He was learning to trim hooves and knock down clenches after the shoes were nailed on, but he doubted if he would ever have the strength to shoe a horse from beginning to end. His one advantage, however, was his feeling for horses. Even Tom had grudgingly admitted that he had a knack. Horses seemed to like him.

And he liked them. There were times, climbing into the loft at night, when he felt that every bone in his body had been bruised by the rigours of the day's work, but there was never a morning after when he didn't feel like getting up. The horses made up for all the cuffs and insults he received from Tom and William. Even if he didn't get to touch one of them all day, he loved being near them; loved their sweet smell and their gentle patience.

A stray dog trotted in from the road and began to snuffle around inside the door. Jack tossed him a moon-shaped hoof-trimming, then shoved the rest of his sweepings up against the coal heap. Tom was sorting through a stack of iron rods, filling the confined space with clattering and ringing. The dog took to its heels. Jack added another shovel of charcoal to the fire and began to work the bellows. He had seen Tom do it with one hand, but it took him all his strength to open them and all his weight bearing down to close them. Like a great beast breathing, they drew in air and whooshed it out again, reddening the coals and causing them to spring into flames. A dozen times Jack heaved them open and squashed them closed and then, panting and sweating but satisfied with the fire, he sat down to take a breather.

'Water, lad. Hop it!'

Jack jumped up and gathered a pair of buckets. He fetched and carried from the pump until he had filled the barrel where the steel was tempered when it had been heated and shaped. Soon afterwards, Nicholson arrived with his smart cob, and Tom set Jack to making nails.

The morning wore on. The sun rose above the line of the buildings opposite and cast bright light through the wide doors of the forge, adding to the heat already spreading from the furnace. Tom's temper began to deteriorate. A pair of carriage horses came in to be shod, and after them came a heavy dray horse with feet the size of dinner plates. Tom sweated and cursed, and began, as usual, to take out his irritation on Jack. He gave him one order after another, to tend the forge, to hand him a hammer, to finish off the clenches. Jack ran from one side of the smithy to the other and Tom scolded him for being slow, and then for not finishing the job he had just pulled him away from. It seemed to Jack that he could do nothing right. He began to get nervous and his nervousness made him clumsy. He spilled a shovelful of charcoal, then spilled it again when he had swept it up. Tom slapped him for it, and made him drop a heavy rasp on to his toe. When he yelled in pain, Tom gave him another slap for alarming the horse he was shoeing. The day that had begun so well was becoming a nightmare.

At noon Tom closed the double doors and sent Jack for bread and herrings for their lunch. They ate in tense silence for a while, then Tom nodded towards the dwindling pile of charcoal.

'You'll have to go for a load,' he said.

'By myself?' said Jack. He had been with William before, down to the docks where the charcoal was brought by boat from the forests upstream, but he had never been allowed to take the reins.

'All you have to do is steer,' said Tom. 'Old Dobbs knows his job. You're not likely to get into any trouble. You know the way, don't you?'

Jack nodded, and slowly his anxiety gave way to delight at the thought of spending the afternoon sitting on a cart, out of the way of Tom and his temper.

'Tack him up, then, lad, and get on the road.' Tom nodded at the charcoal pile again. 'We might even need it before the day's out.'

In the stable at the side of the yard, the old pony stood dozing, oblivious to the clouds of flies which buzzed around his eyes. Jack dragged out the collar and harness and tried to fit them on the pony. It looked so simple when William did it but now, faced with a dozen different straps and buckles, Jack realised that he had no idea how it all worked. He was afraid to ask Tom for help, but the harder he tried to fit the harness, the more bewildered he became. When Tom came out to see what was taking so long, he flew into a rage. He shoved Jack so hard against the stable wall that the wind was knocked out of him. It hurt, but it hurt more to see Tom taking out his anger on the patient old pony. He flung the harness on to him, yanking at the straps with all his brutal strength. Dobbs threw up his head and grunted, then followed the blacksmith at a trot out into the yard, where he was rammed backwards between the shafts of the cart.

Jack ran through the smithy to open the doors, then climbed up on to the seat and picked up the reins. Tom thrust a shilling into his hand. 'And mind you don't take all day, you hear? Or I'll show you what real trouble means!'

Dobbs trotted along nervously for the first few minutes, driven by the memory of the blacksmith's fury. But when, after a while, he realised that he was safe, he slowed to a jog, then a walk. The empty cart rattled along the rutted cobbles. Around them, the streets were busy with people; life going on outside now that the weather was so fine. Small children carried smaller ones on their hips while their mothers did what work could be done outside. Doors and shutters stood open, the interiors behind them cast into deep gloom by the brilliance of the summer light. Washing hung from every available hook and ledge. A thousand smells, some good, some bad, rose from the city streets and met and mingled in the air. Jack was proud to be riding through it all in charge of a pony and cart, even if they were both a bit wobbly and worn.

Dobbs, recognising that Jack had no authority, had slowed to an idle, dawdling pace. He took interest in very little that happened, though he would occasionally raise his head in curiosity if they passed another horse. Jack made a few futile attempts to hurry him along, then gave up. It didn't seem fair, somehow. The pony was old; slack and bony. His bay coat was dull, and his soft, brown eyes were hollow with endurance. Jack knew that he wasn't the first apprentice to have served time behind Dobbs' slow-swinging rump, but he suspected that he might be the last. A sudden fear sprang up that the pony might just fold up between the shafts and not rise again. He had seen it once before with a cart-horse not far from his home. He remembered the light fading out of the old eyes as the horse died, and was afraid of it happening again, and of seeing Dobbs reproach him.

But he wouldn't, if he understood. In many ways Jack's life had been even harder than the pony's. He shook the reins, feeling suddenly restless. He didn't like thinking about things that made him uncomfortable. It was one of the reasons he loved the smithy so much, despite Tom's temper. He was always busy with one thing or another. There was never any empty time to sit around and reflect upon the series of misfortunes that constituted his existence, or to contemplate what possible future a boy like himself might expect.

Chapter Two

WHEN Jack arrived at the quayside where he and William had previously collected charcoal, there was nothing to be seen but a large area of black dust on the flagstones. He pulled Dobbs to a halt and looked around. He remembered the river wall to be a busy place, with boats drawing in regularly to load or unload, but now it was remarkably quiet.

Dobbs swished his short tail listlessly and rested a hind leg. Jack looped the reins around the front rail of the cart and slipped down on to the ground. The river smelled foul in the afternoon heat and it was with a slight feeling of distaste that Jack approached the quay. Two men were sitting on a pile of sacks, but there was no activity. There didn't even seem to be any boats.

'Looking for something?' one of the men called.

'Charcoal,' said Jack.

'It's there all right,' said the man. 'Over there, see?'

Jack followed his pointing finger to a small boat at anchor in the middle of the river, and now he saw what the problem was. The tide, which backed up the river from the sea, was right out. A long spell of dry weather had left the water level low and there was no way that any boat could unload until the tide lifted it up nearer to the level of the docks.

'Will it be long?' he asked.

'No. Not too long.'

Jack sat down on the warm stone of the river wall and dangled his legs over the side. The water was so low that a pair of swans near the opposite bank were grazing the river-bed, dipping their long necks and emerging with mouths full of slimy green weed. Beneath him, a little further upstream, another boat was sitting on its keel, listing over away from the wall. Jack sighed and settled down to wait.

He had no way of knowing how fast or how slowly the afternoon was passing. The two men settled themselves down on their bulging sacks and went to sleep, but Jack could find no release from the gruelling pressure of wasted time. The swans finished their meal and swam on, out of sight. Occasionally a fish jumped and broke the murky surface of the water. Most of the time there was nothing.

Jack's anxiety increased with every minute that passed. It didn't matter that he wasn't to blame for the delay. He was going to be in trouble with Tom, and the longer he was away, the worse the trouble would be. By the time he thought of going back to the forge, he had already left it too late and the tide was beginning to come in. But it was slow, much slower than he had expected. The sun dipped behind the houses on the opposite bank and an evening feel crept into the air. The two men were joined by two more, who woke them up. Their boat was rising up the side of the wall now, and after a leisurely conversation, they shortened the painter and began to lower the sacks into the hold.

Still the charcoal boat did not come in. Jack was joined by another cart and a handful of women and children with buckets and baskets, all waiting in cheerful companionship. Jack wished he felt half as cheerful. He could feel Tom's anger already.

Eventually the boat lifted anchor and was punted across the current and tied up. It was still a good deal lower than the top of the wall but the crew seemed to have decided that the water level was about as high as it would get. The coals were shovelled into large, soft baskets, which were hauled up on to the quayside. The number of waiting customers seemed to double with the arrival of the boat, and they joined in, hurrying the work along. Jack moved forward to help, trying to get his cart loaded and away, but he hadn't a chance. Everyone else seemed bigger and stronger than he was. He was shouldered out of the way time after time, with the result that instead of being first, he was one of the last to get his load. By that time, most of the others had gone. He brought the patient Dobbs up close to the dock, but he couldn't lift the baskets up to the height of the cart and had to empty them on to the ground and shovel up the charcoal from there.

It was back-breaking work. The little cart seemed to be bottomless, the shovel both too small and too heavy. Further along the wall, the men finished loading their sacks and went home. The crew set full sails and the boat drifted languidly upriver before a light breeze. Jack wished he was on it. He had never been out of London. Up the river, he knew, were fields and farms and open countryside. His mother had been born among them somewhere, but he could only guess what they looked like.

When, at last, the coals began to roll back down from the top of the heap in the cart, Jack stopped and slung the shovel underneath the driver's bench. He paid the boatmen, climbed up behind Dobbs' scrawny rump and shook the reins.

The pony set off willingly, eager to get home. He knew the way better than Jack did and took each turn without any prompting. The streets were quieter now, smelling of smoke and cooking, making Jack hungry. He was hot from his work, and he took off his shirt. He was tired, too. Very tired.

'Whoa! Whoa there in the cart!'

The shout jolted him awake, but it was too late. Dobbs seemed to be asleep as well, ambling along between the shafts. His head was lolling on a level with his knees, and no matter how hard Jack hauled on the reins he would neither stop nor turn back on to his own side of the street. There was nothing that anyone could do.

It was not a dramatic accident. The speed of Dobbs' progress was minimal and the horse pulling the other cart was more attentive and had already stopped. There was a grinding crunch as the two wheel-hubs encountered each other. Dobbs, eager to get home, leant into the battered collar of his harness despite Jack's opposition and turned a minor delay into a disaster. Jack's wheel hub rolled up over the other. The weight of the charcoal caused its rusted iron cover to shear and bite deeply into the bare wood of the bigger, newer wheel, locking the two together. Dobbs admitted defeat and relaxed.

Jack dropped the reins and covered his face with his hands as the cart driver jumped down and came round to examine the problem.

People began to drift out of the nearby houses to see what was happening. A young man on his way home from work with a bag of tools slipped in between the carts and looked on, scratching his breast-bone. Dobbs stood four square, leaning into his collar slightly as though he was trying to take the weight off his feet. Jack looked up, just in time to see a couple of boys of about his own age filching pieces of charcoal from his load. He yelled at them and they backed away, giggling.

The other driver walked up beside Jack. He was a tall man and heavy set, with a slight squint which made Jack uncertain about where exactly he was looking.

'Back up,' he said. There was an underlying threat in his voice which reminded Jack of Tom, and the nightmare still to be faced. He gathered the reins and hauled on them. Dobbs put his head up and opened his mouth, but continued to lean towards home and the armful of sweet hay that would be waiting there.

'I said pull him back!'

Jack heaved again. 'I'm trying!' he said. 'He won't come.'

The man gritted his teeth and shook his head. He kicked the iron rim of the near wheel. 'Who does this contraption belong to?'

'Tom Bradley,' said Jack, still pulling fruitlessly at the reins. The young workman stepped forward and took hold of the bridle.

'Go back,' he said, pushing hard on the pony's nose. But Dobbs just dropped his dusty old forehead against the newcomer's chest as though seeking refuge from the confusion.

'I'll give that Tom Bradley something to think about if I catch him,' said the other driver, moving back towards the pony's head. 'What does he think he's up to, sending children on his errands?'

'I'm not a child! I'm fourteen!' Jack's voice was high, strangled with emotion.

'And a liar as well!' The workman stepped back as the bigger man snatched the reins from him and clouted Dobbs squarely on the nose. Dobbs recoiled into the traces and began to back up.

'Get off him!' Jack stood up, ready to jump down to the pony's defence. There was a grinding sound as the cartwheels scrunched across the cobbles, both vehicles swivelling around the axis of the joined hubs.

'Whoa, whoa!' called one of the onlookers. 'It's no good!'

The men left Dobbs alone and went to look. If anything, the effort had made things worse. Some other solution would have to be found.

The young workman turned out to be a carpenter. He spent some time with his tool bag, trying to prise the hubs apart, but nothing came of it. After that, a few men from the growing crowd joined in, and there were several attempts to lift Jack's cart off the other one. At every failed attempt, the big man let fly a new hail of abuse at Jack and his carelessness, until Jack became immune to it and turned a deaf ear. Someone suggested that the charcoal be off-loaded, but Jack pleaded for sympathy and the idea was forgotten. There was renewed discussion among the huddle of men around the wheels, with a great deal of nodding and shaking of heads. Everyone took it in turns to bend down close and inspect the situation. Then someone made a swinging motion with both hands together through the air. There was a long pause, followed by a unified murmur of assent. The carpenter left his tool bag under Jack's seat and ran off down the street.

The other driver glowered at Jack and went back to his cart. Everyone seemed to be waiting for something, but Jack didn't dare ask what it was. After a while the excitement of the situation wore off and people began to wander back down the street and into their houses. The few who stayed on relaxed and chatted cosily in the warm evening. A woman took pity on Jack and brought him a muffin from her house. He ate it gratefully as he waited.

When the carpenter eventually returned, he was carrying a sledgehammer over his shoulder. Jack's heart sank. The other driver took it and swung it a few times, feeling its weight.

'Jump down, lad,' he said to Jack. 'Go and stand at the pony's head.'

There was some more discussion then, about where the blow should be aimed, and how hard it should be struck. Jack stroked Dobbs' nose and spoke to him quietly. The carpenter came and joined him, taking the other side of the bridle, just in case.

There was no need. The old pony had seen and heard everything. Nothing scared him any more. When the blow came, the carthorse jumped and skittered, sending up sparks from the cobbles, but Dobbs barely pricked an ear. Jack would have been proud of him, had his attention not been taken by the disaster that was happening between the two carts. The sledge blow had freed the wheels, but Tom's cart hadn't withstood it. Beneath its iron cap, the wooden hub was old and decayed. It caved in under the pressure and, deprived of their anchorage, the spokes clattered out on to the road. The wooden rim collapsed inwards and the outer, iron one fell over with a clang as the axle of the cart dropped to the ground.

The silence that followed was broken only by a small landslide of charcoal which bounced and rolled among the cobbles. For a long time after it had settled, no one spoke. The big man stared, his good eye on the broken wheel and the other on the horizon. His mouth was open in horror at what he had done, but a moment later he closed it again.

'It was full of worms,' he said self-righteously, kicking one of the redundant spokes out of the road. 'And the pony is, too, by the look of things.'

'And the boy,' called the woman who had given Jack the muffin. Everyone laughed, except for Jack. The big man led his horse clear of the wreckage and climbed up on to the seat of his cart.

'You'd better run and get your master,' he said. But Jack was stuck to the cobbles where he stood. How could he leave the cart and its load abandoned in the middle of the street? And what about Dobbs? The old pony was hanging his head, utterly dejected.

Jack looked up. There was still light but stars were appearing in it, seed crystals around which the night was beginning to thicken. Birds and bats were in the air together, wheeling above the chimneys, changing the watch. There was something ominous about their joint sovereignty of the skies and Jack shivered. His shirt was tied by the sleeves around his waist. He didn't remember putting it there. As he fumbled with the knot he felt, rather than heard, the high voice of a bat which swooped for a moth above his head. Something gave way in his mind. The effects of the catastrophe came rolling in upon his imagination. He would suffer for what he had done. Tom would thrash the daylights out of him, and that would be the least of it. It was over, his apprenticeship in the hot forge. No more bellows, no more sweet smell of horses. There would be no second chances for him, a puny, rickety boy with nothing but failure behind him.

The other cart was moving off, the young horse striding jauntily, delighted to be moving again. Dobbs sighed in the lop-sided traces. The carpenter rubbed his dusty neck kindly and began to untack him.

'You can ride him home, lad,' he said. 'I'll keep an eye on the cart until your master gets here.'

But he was talking to no one. Jack was gone.

Chapter Three

HE was running as fast as his bowed legs would carry him, going nowhere except away from his own disaster. He ran down lanes which grew narrower and darker until they turned into the stinking pig-alleys of the poorest parts of the city, where the truffled-up refuse was churned into a black slime which oozed between his toes. His body was stiff from shovelling, and his lungs didn't seem deep enough to contain the air that he needed, but still he kept running. Tom seemed to be at his shoulder no matter where he turned, and the abandoned Dobbs, who he loved better than anyone, would never look at him again.

At last he had to stop. His body was trembling from overexertion and he was panting like a dog. Light spangled his vision, but it was only a trick of his racing blood. When it cleared, he was in darkness. Around him the small decrepit houses were slowly crumbling into decay. Their mud and straw faces were scarred and pock-marked. They gazed blandly at Jack from shutterless windows and he stood mesmerised until a child somewhere coughed and cried, reminding him that he was still alive.

He walked on, half dreaming. His knees shook and buckled with exhaustion, but he kept moving until, to his surprise, he found himself at the river again. It wasn't the docks where he had been earlier in the day, but he knew the place all the same. To his left was the ruin of an ancient monastery, its halls and cells and cloisters open to the stars above. Long before Jack's time it had been plundered and left abandoned. As he looked at it now, he wasn't sure what its original purpose had been, though he remembered that someone had once explained it to him. He was in no doubt, however, about its present use. The beggars from the whole of the eastern side of the city had colonised it. No one knew how many. Inside, he had been told, the beggars erected lean-tos against the solid stone walls and thatched them with rushes and straw. They cooked beneath the open skies and slept huddled together to keep warm. The monastery was a law unto itself, a miniature state within the confines of the city. It had its own rules and customs, and the inhabitants had divided the surrounding parishes among themselves. Any stranger discovered intruding upon their territory was quickly repelled. The monastery beggars did not readily admit newcomers.

Jack crept past the old cloister walls and looked down into the water. The tide was receding again. The river slithered along on its bed, slow in the darkness, slimy as a slug. There was no sound from the monastery, but Jack felt exposed and walked cautiously along the coping stones until he came to a flight of deep steps which led down to the river bed. In days gone by, boats had moored there to unload provisions for the monks, but not recently; not since the beggars had taken over. Jack walked down four steps and sat on the fifth with his back against the wall. He was hidden there, as safe as he could be in the circumstances. His race through the alleys had warmed him, but the cold stone against his back reminded him of the shirt still clutched in his hand. As he put it on, he became aware of how tattered it was. He had seen better-dressed beggars. Perhaps it was no coincidence that his feet had brought him here, to their door. All that separated him from them was his apprenticeship; the hope that it offered of some future security. Now even that was gone.

Jack dreamt that he was at home in his bed beside the hearth. He woke in the first light of dawn, explaining to his mother that the cock hadn't crowed yet; it still wasn't time to get up. She didn't answer him. He opened his eyes.

The first thing he saw was a sheep's heart bobbing on the rising tide at the foot of the steps. It was nothing unusual. The river was always full of offal. It was his being there at all that surprised him. He looked round. He was bitterly cold. His body was locked at an awkward angle. He turned over, trying to get back to the warm ashes of his mother's fire, his hand groping for the horse-hair blanket that smelled of himself and home and comfort. It wasn't there.

He rubbed his eyes and sat up, his body stiff and sore. The sky was blue-grey and the stars were dissolving, taking the darkness with them. In the water below, the sheep's heart was still lolling on the gentle waves which washed against the steps. There was something strange about the way it was floating. From the beggar colony came a whiff of wood smoke and the bleat of a goat. Jack wondered what it lived on. Above him, a single gull was circling, assessing him with a hostile eye. As he glared back at it, the realisation came, as if from nowhere, that the thing in the water was not a sheep's heart. He looked back quickly. It was still there, inching its way downstream.

Jack jumped up and ran down to catch it before it could be tempted out into the current. As he put a hand to it, he knew that he was right. It was not flesh at all but hard as bone and about the same weight. He turned it over in his hands. The cool water dripped between his fingers on to the threadbare knees of his trousers. He searched through his memory for clues, but nothing came. He had never seen anything remotely like this before.

It was hollow and roughly spherical, of some hard material like pottery or pewter, but not exactly either of them. A tube branched out of the top, which was why Jack had first thought that it was a sheep's heart. As he looked more closely, he saw that the tube, or spout, had been sealed with some sort of black, resinous material. Whatever the thing was, someone had made it.

'What you got?'

Jack whipped round, instinctively keeping the object hidden behind his body. Above him, on the river wall, a man was standing. He was barefoot and bare legged. If he was wearing any clothes above his knees Jack couldn't tell, since he was wrapped in a torn and grimy blanket tucked up around his chin. His hair was long and matted and a thick beard covered his face almost entirely. But his eyes shone through and made Jack's blood run cold.

'You got something. What is it?'

'Nothing,' said Jack, turning his back again. 'Just an old sheep's heart.' He was pressing his new find so hard against his waist that it was hurting him. Nothing would induce him to part with it.

'Give it here.'

'It's rotten. What do you want it for?'

There was a long silence. The hairs on the back of Jack's neck stood up as he imagined the terrifying figure slipping down the steps behind him. He dared not turn round. Somehow he knew that if his fear showed in his face, he was lost. When the man finally spoke again, Jack let out his breath in a flood of relief. He was still standing on the river wall.

'For my dog,' he said.

Jack squatted down on the step, his back still turned. The last high tide had washed some pieces of driftwood up on to the lower steps. Surreptitiously, he picked one up. It was small, but soggy, the perfect weight. Without being sure why he was doing it, he tossed it out into the current, where it sent up a satisfying splash.

There was another long silence before the man spoke again.

'What you do that for?'

'It was rotten.'

'Little swine. I'll teach you.'

Jack's knees were trembling. He bent down and began to toss the other pieces of driftwood into the river, his blood roaring so loud in his ears that he couldn't hear the splashes they made. His only chance, he knew, was the expression of absolute calm and disdain. When all the wood was gone there was no sound from the river wall above him. At any moment he expected to feel the clutch of a clammy hand on the back of his neck, but he couldn't turn to look. His senses seemed to be frozen behind him, but to turn would be to betray himself. Then suddenly, without knowing why, he was certain that the danger had passed.

He turned round. The wall above him was empty.

Jack was triumphant. The ordeal was over and he had emerged victorious. He swaggered around on the step and sneered at the suspicious seagull. The first rays of the sun broke over the ruined walls behind him, and in their brighter light he bent again to examine the object he had found and defended. As he did so, his spirits sank. He had no idea what it was or whether it had any value. Perhaps his possessiveness had been about nothing. Far from being over, his ordeal was only just beginning.

There was more smoke from the monastery. Jack could see it now, tumbling out over the broken walls, searching for direction in the motionless air. Soon the beggars would be emerging and spreading out over the city. Jack had no wish to meet with them. Stealthily he climbed up the steps and, seeing that the road was clear, set off along it. He didn't run, since running would be sure to arouse curiosity, but he walked as fast as he could. His rickety legs caused him to roll along on the outsides of his feet, which had developed hard skin like a second sole. There were times when it embarrassed him and he wished he was like other, stronger boys, but as he bowled along beside the river he had no awareness of it at all. All his attention was on the little pot that he still held clutched against his belly. He was unsure how to hold it. As it was, held openly in his hand, someone who knew what it was might recognise it and demand it from him or accuse him of theft. But if he tried to conceal it beneath his shirt he was likely to draw even more attention to himself. After long deliberation he decided to hold it by its tube. His hand concealed it, and the earth-coloured bulb that protruded was unlikely to arouse much curiosity.

By the time he had adjusted it to his satisfaction and assumed a carefully innocent expression, the city was well awake. A milkman passed, leading two mules loaded with cans. Jack remembered the taste of sweet milk and briefly considered trying to swap the pot for a dipper of it. But before he could decide, the milkman and his lop-eared followers had gone past him. They didn't seem to notice him at all. It was only then that Jack began to think about where he was going.

His feet had been carrying him towards his own part of town; where his mother used to live, within a few streets of

Tom Bradley's forge. There was no future for him there; no one could afford to take him in and feed him, but he needed to find someone who could tell him what to do. The pot looked common and worthless, a drab old thing, growing slippery with sweat in his grip, and yet there was something about it that excited him. He had to find out whether or not it had any value before he could decide on his next step, and he could think of no one to turn to apart from his old neighbours. At least one of them would be sure to know.

The street pumps were busy as the town began the new day. Queues formed beside them as people washed themselves, sloshed out chamber pots, filled buckets for their animals. Sleepy tradesmen pushed handcarts loaded with bread, onions, fish. Goats were milked, dogs were kicked, horses were tackled and chickens were fed on the cobbles, among the feet of children playing in the morning sun. If anyone noticed Jack and his unusual possession they didn't see fit to challenge him, and as he drew near to his own neighbourhood he was both relieved and a little disappointed.

He began to meet with people that knew him.

'Where you going, Jack?'

'What's that you have there?'

He answered all the questions the same way, with a smile and a shrug. No one bothered to press him. But as he was approaching the lane where he had once lived, a hand reached out and grabbed him by the forearm. A small girl, rickety as himself, was making fearsome faces at him.

'Stop! Watch yourself, Jack!'

'Why? What's up, Sally?'

'You're in big trouble. Didn't you know that?'

He did know, of course he did. How had he managed to forget?

Sally led him cautiously to the corner of the lane. The house there had been built of uncut stone, and the walls bulged and receded in a parody of symmetry. Jack and Sally crouched behind the huge, jutting cornerstone, a boulder which had probably stood just where it was long before the city had grown up around it.

'What you got?' the girl asked.

'Shh!' said Jack, peering out. A few doors down the lane, his mother's neighbour, Peg, was standing in her doorway. Beside her, his back turned towards Jack, was the brawny figure of Tom Bradley. He had rolled his sleeves up above his elbows, as he always did when there was some particularly heavy work about to be done. In one hand he held a broken spoke. The other arm was raised and planted against the lime-washed wall above Peg's head.

'What is it?' Sally was saying, tugging at the object in Jack's hand.

'Leave it, will you?' Jack snatched it away.

'Did you steal it or what?'

Down the lane, Peg was shaking her head gravely. Her neighbours were standing around at a discreet distance, but all within earshot.

'What you going to do with it, Jack?'

'Shh!'

'You going to sell it?'

Peg and Tom were nodding together and, with a sudden sense of horror, Jack understood that they were allies. Peg wasn't defending him against the blacksmith's wrath, she was in agreement with him. There was no one now, no one in the world who would shelter him. He felt suddenly, desperately alone.

Tom shifted his weight and turned to look up the lane. Jack ducked rapidly behind the cornerstone, but Sally had lost all awareness of the danger.

'You going to bring it to Nancy?' she said. 'Can I come with you?'

Jack didn't answer. Shaking free of the girl, he got up and ran back the way he had come. But this time he didn't go far. Despite her irritating curiosity, Sally had been useful. Not only had she saved Jack from walking straight into a trap, she had also given him an idea that he might not have come up with himself.

Nancy.

Chapter Four

THE market was a dangerous place for Jack to be. He was there nearly every day, running one sort of errand or another, and most of the stall holders knew him by name. Although he had no way of knowing whether Tom had put the word out about him, he was certain that everyone would have heard about the abandoned pony and cart, and that it would soon get back to the blacksmith if he was seen. So instead of walking through the centre, he arrived by way of the back lanes and alleys. This brought him out at the end of one of the side streets that radiated outwards from the market square.

These streets were never too busy. The stalls which lined them offered specialist wares which people didn't need every day. Shoemakers set up on low stools with their lasts and tools spread out in front of them. Tailors patched and altered and occasionally got an order for a new garment. New pots and pans could be bought from the ironmongers in the square, but out here, tinkers mended old ones. Beside them, men with whetstones sharpened knives and scissors and shears. Bakers passed through with trays of penny loaves, and among them all, children dodged and begged and thieved.

Nancy was well known to every one of them, and to many more besides. Her little stall at the top of the street sold anything old that had any use left in it at all. She sold dented ladles and bent spoons and billy-cans ten times mended. She sold chipped chamber pots, buckets without handles, bits of rusted harness, twig brooms, butter churns. Best of all, for the hungry children of the town, she sold buttons and buckles and bootlaces, hooks and handles and hairpins, needles, thimbles, harness rings; all those small things that got dropped from time to time around the place and could be found by sharp eyes and retrieved by nimble fingers. A good collection of things might earn a small coin, but in general Nancy paid her suppliers with a piece of toffee or a pickled onion or, in the season, a plum or an apple. No one, whether they were buying or selling, ever left Nancy's stall feeling cheated. She was known throughout the entire city. If it wasn't to be found anywhere else, Nancy was sure to have it.

She was there as usual, sitting broadly on a chair with three and a half legs and no back. Jack waited, hugging the shadows of a workshop door until a couple of women who were browsing through boxes of oddments got bored and wandered on to the basket maker on the next stall. Then he darted over and slipped in between Nancy's stout knee and a stack of boxes filled with dented pewter. Nancy whooped with surprise, then burst out laughing.

'Gracious, Jack. What will you be up to next?'

Jack put a finger to his lips and shook his head.

'On the run?' said Nancy. 'Not you, Jack, surely? Who from?'

Again Jack made a plea for silence, but Nancy was not to be deterred.

'You just tell me, lad. I'll teach them something they never knew about widows.'

Nancy made boxing motions in the air in front of her face. She made no secret of the fact that widowhood was the best thing that had happened in her life. In the ten years since her husband died, she had changed from a subdued servant into a successful businesswoman. She welcomed the attentions of the many bachelors who took a remarkable interest in her wares, but if they tried to get too close she wasted no time in setting them straight. Nancy was her own woman and had no intention of ever becoming anyone else's again.

Jack despaired of shutting her up and, instead, held up the object he had found. It had the desired effect. A puzzled expression came over Nancy's face. She took it from Jack and turned it round in her fingers.

'What is it?' she whispered.

Jack's heart sank. 'Don't you know?'

Nancy shook her head, then giggled. 'It reminds me a bit

of a certain gentleman I used to know . . .' She stopped, seeing the disheartened expression on Jack's face. 'No, no,' she went on, her voice becoming quite serious. 'I'm sure it's something. Let me see now.' For a long time she examined the mysterious pot, turning it this way and that, shaking it, polishing it with spit. She was kind to her suppliers and would gladly have sent Jack away with a handful of the raspberries that were under the stall, but she had a feeling that he expected more than that. Since she had no idea of what the thing was worth, she couldn't make him an offer.

A customer came and, after much haggling, bought two short lengths of chain. When he had gone, the cogs of Nancy's mind were beginning to turn.

'It has to be something,' she said, turning it round and sniffing at it. 'Where did you find it?'

'In the river.'

'Where in the river?'

'Beside the monastery.'

Nancy's mind was engaged in such profound concentration that Jack feared for her. Then, suddenly, it happened. She looked up and met his eyes with a fierce certainty.

'I know what it is.'

Butterflies danced under Jack's ribcage. 'Do you?'

'I do,' said Nancy. 'It's a relic.'

'A what?'

'A relic. That's definitely what it is.'

'Then what's it worth?' Hope created a terrible pressure in Jack's chest.

'I can't say,' said Nancy, 'because I don't deal in relics. But I can tell you who does and you can go there yourself and find out.'

She stood up and pointed across the street, not at the houses on the other side but straight through them, as if they weren't there. 'You have to cross over by London Bridge and go out of the city towards Dulwich. When you get there, you can ask anyone for Master Gregory's house and they'll tell you the way.'

'Is it outside London?' said Jack.

'Of course it is. Haven't you been there before?'

Jack shook his head. 'Never.'

'Well, it's about time you did, then. You'll have no trouble as long as you mind your manners. People are the same everywhere. And you'll enjoy the countryside. It's beautiful in this kind of weather.'

Jack nodded and retrieved the pot from Nancy. 'Will Master Gregory buy it from me?'

'Depends if it's a good relic or not. I know he likes old ones.'

'It looks old,' said Jack.

Nancy reached into a basket beside her knee and pulled out a bundle wrapped in flannel. Inside it was a small loaf of bread and a pair of pigs' trotters. She gave Jack one of them and half the loaf.

'Now get on, before you waste any more of my good time.' Her voice was stern, but she was smiling. 'And don't tell anyone where you got that or they'll all be here looking for some.'

Jack chewed the trotter down to the bone as he walked along beside the river, but didn't throw it away. It was still good to gnaw on. Above his head, gulls were flying purposefully upriver, heading away from some unseen storm at sea. The people he passed along the way seemed to share their apprehension, hurrying about their business, answering his requests for directions curtly. An occasional cool gust blew in from the estuary, causing Jack to wonder whether he ought not to turn back and wait for another day to make the journey. He might have, had there been anywhere for him to return to.

He crossed London Bridge with the relic held by its neck in one hand and the pig's trotter in the other. The day was as hot as the one before, but in a different way. A low bank of cloud had moved in and the air was damp and close. Jack's clothes were sticky against his skin.

His path led him away from the river, and in a surprisingly short time the crowded streets gave way to open countryside. For a while, Jack forgot everything, entranced by the scenery. It wasn't that he had never seen such things; there were trees in the city, and grass, and vegetable gardens. But to see a hundred trees together and whole eyefuls of green and yellow grasses took his breath away. He had seen cows before, and sheep penned up beside the butcher's, but he had never seen them where they belonged, grazing freely on green commonage, placid and fat. There were no gulls or pigeons, but the hedgerows were alive with small brown birds which fluttered out of his way, then burst into song behind him. The horizon was immeasurably distant; nothing except the sky had ever seemed so far away and it felt as though his eyes had to stretch to look at it. It was all so different that it made him uncomfortable, smaller than ever amongst such largeness. And yet it excited him. He had the impression that he had lived in a box all his life and had just discovered how to open the lid.

Despite its vastness, the countryside was very far from empty. All along the way, farmers and labourers were working flat out, desperate to save the hay and thatch the ricks before the rain arrived. On two occasions, Jack was called upon to lend a hand. He didn't like to refuse, but he was reluctant to display his ignorance, and even more reluctant to undertake anything which would require him to let go of his precious pot, even for a short time. So both times he pretended he hadn't heard and passed on along his way between ripening orchards and cottage gardens, everything bursting with life.

It was early afternoon when Jack arrived in Dulwich. The village street was long and narrow, and surprisingly empty. The only activity Jack could find was at the forge, where a small crowd of waiting customers had gathered, watching the blacksmith repair the axle of a hay-wagon. Jack approached a boy who was holding a broken pitchfork. It looked as if he would have a long wait but he seemed happy enough, despite the urgency in the surrounding countryside.

'What you want to go there for?' he said, when Jack asked him for directions to Master Gregory's house.

Jack folded his arms across the relic. The trotter bone was still in his hand. 'I have a message for him.'

'From who?'

Jack made to move away, to ask someone less curious, but the boy reached out and took him by the arm.

'See the tall sycamore, there? Turn in just beside it, through the iron gates.'

'How will I know the house?'

'You can't miss it. There's only one house. What you got there, anyway?'

'Nothing.'

The boy let go of Jack's arm and shrugged. 'I don't care. Go there if you want. He's mad, though. Did you know that?'

Jack looked over towards the sycamore tree. The boy laughed sneeringly and twisted a finger at his temple. 'Mad as a March hare,' he said.

The iron gates were wide enough to admit two carts side by side, if not three. They swung soundlessly on well-oiled hinges as Jack went through. As he walked timidly along the broad, tree-lined avenue, he thought about what the boy had said. In what way was Gregory mad? Was he mad like the drunkards who rolled outside his mother's door in the early hours of the morning, laughing at the moon and shouting at ghosts? Or was he staring mad like the man who had challenged Jack when he first found the relic down beside the river? And if he was mad, how could he have money?

Red squirrels dashed through the branches above Jack's head, and a bright green woodpecker with a red head dipped across the open space of the drive. Anything could happen here, in a place like this. It was like a dream after the drabness of London. And it became even more like a dream when he turned a bend in the drive and saw the horses. They were standing in a smooth, green paddock beneath huge oak trees and they were like no horses that Jack had ever seen. Even though the sky was full of clouds, their coats shone like new conkers. There were bays and browns and chestnuts, the colours fresh and bright against the sweet green of the pasture. Foals lay flat on the grass, motionless apart from the occasional twitch of a fuzzy tail. Jack crept up to the paddock rail, with eyes for nothing but the horses. The mares surveyed him with mild interest, nodding their heads against the flies. He clucked and called to them softly, pleading with them to come, but they ignored him.

A sound behind Jack made him turn. He had been so intent upon the horses as he rounded the bend that he hadn't looked the other way at all. Behind him, a sheet was flapping out of the open window of the biggest house he had ever seen. It was the length of his own lane in the city and four times as high as his mother's house. The sheet was gathered in again by the maid who was airing it and the window closed behind her.

Had she seen him? Was she running now to set the dogs on to him? There had clearly been some mistake. No dealer ever lived in a house like this, not even a dealer in relics. Either Nancy had been mistaken or that stupid farmer's boy had given him the wrong directions as a joke.

Chapter Five

THE long-threatened rain started to fall in big, warm drops. Small patches appeared on the stones of the driveway, then spread into each other until the whole area changed colour. The foals woke and sniffed the air, then got up and ran to their mothers to feed. The shower became heavier and thunder rolled in the distance. Through the deluge the house looked even more forbidding than before, but as Jack was despairing of ever finding the courage to approach it, a strange thing happened. The rare and delightful smell of the thirsty earth rose up through the air and wrapped itself around him, as warm and comforting as his favourite blanket. All of a sudden he knew that Nancy would never make a fool of him. She would not have sent him all this way for nothing.

He slipped along beside the paddocks and around the side of the house. The stable yard which formed a square against the rear wall of the house was empty. The doors of the loose boxes stood open. Nothing moved, not even, to Jack's relief, a dog. The rain was falling hard, making balls out of the dust and sending them scudding across the yard. The drain pipes which ran down the walls were just beginning to gurgle and drip.

Jack was soaked to the skin. As he approached the back door his clothes felt too tight for him and his heart seemed restricted inside his chest. He intended to knock with confidence, but his fist made a thin, timid little sound on the heavy wooden panels. There were mutterings and scufflings from within, then a tall, lean woman opened the door. She greeted Jack with a look of mild irritation and said, 'Wait there.'

Jack waited. A moment later the woman returned with a small crust of bread. Jack found that he was still holding the remains of the pig's knuckle. The woman prized it out of his fingers and threw it aside with an expression of distaste. The bread she replaced it with was so stale that it was sharp.

'I don't want it,' Jack said.

'Well, it's all you're going to get!' As she spoke, the housekeeper was already closing the door in Jack's face.

'I got a relic!' he shouted.

The door opened again.

'Look.' Jack held it up.

The look of irritation on the woman's face intensified, but again she asked him to wait while she disappeared inside.

She was gone longer this time. A fat spaniel emerged from somewhere or other and slunk away towards the outhouses with the trotter bone. The doorway sheltered Jack from the worst of the rain, but his wet clothes were uncomfortable and, worse than that, they were beginning to release odours that even he was aware of. He would have been due a bath and a change of clothes if he had been at home. He wished he was. He wished that none of it had ever happened.

The door opened at last.

'In you come.'

The housekeeper led the way through a dark hallway into the fuggy heat of a huge kitchen, where a kettle on a black hob steamed softly like a purring cat.

'Go on up,' she said, settling herself into a chair at a long scrubbed table and taking up where she had left off, podding a large bowl of peas. Jack watched her for a while, then said, 'Up where?'

'Have you not been here before?'

'No.'

Some of the peas were maggoty. The housekeeper continued to separate them for a while in silence, then sighed like old Dobbs and stood up again. Wiping her hands on her apron, she led the way out of the kitchen and into a flagstoned hall that was as big as Tom's forge. Dark paintings and faded tapestries lined its walls and Jack stood gaping for a moment or two, then followed the housekeeper up a flight of solid wooden stairs which doubled back on themselves and led to a large, bright landing. Several corridors led off it, and in one of them a door stood slightly ajar. The housekeeper knocked on it, shoved Jack inside, and was gone.

The room was bigger than any Jack had seen. It was bigger and higher than the whole of his mother's house. The two longer walls were lined with shelves and tables and cases with glass tops. At the opposite end, three tall windows were set into the shorter wall, and in front of them was a long, high desk. A man was sitting there with his back towards the door. As Jack came in, he twisted round to look at him.

'Come along,' he said. 'Don't be shy.' His voice bounced hollowly from the walls and the bare floorboards, emphasising the dense silence that followed it. Jack was aware that his clothes were dripping on to the floor. He moved forward. The other end of the room seemed a great distance away. The man turned his chair sideways on and waited. He had the pallor of someone who rarely feels fresh air against his skin, and dark bruises of weariness hung beneath his eyes. His drooping moustache and heavy jowls gave him an air of sadness which surprised Jack. He had always assumed that wealth and happiness were the same thing.

'You have something for me?'

'A relic,' said Jack, stepping forward.

Master Gregory peered at the stale crust in the boy's hand with an expression of bewilderment. Jack held up the other hand with the pot in it.

'Ah, yes,' said Master Gregory. 'Now I see.'

'Is it?' said Jack.

'Is it what?'

'A relic.'

'Let me see it, will you?'

When Jack released his grip, his fingers were cramped into claws from clutching on to his treasure for so long. He stuck the offensive crust into his wet pocket and began to rub his knuckles, without once taking his eyes from the rich man's face. But if there were any clues, Jack was unable to read them. Gregory's face remained quite impassive as he examined the object from every conceivable angle. At last he put it down, very gently, on the desk. For a long moment he sat completely still, as though deep in thought. Then he said, 'What's your name, boy?'

'Jack, sir.'

'Jack. I see. And where did you find this, Jack?'

'In the river, sir.'

'Where, in the river?'

'Blackfriars, sir. Beside the old monastery.'

Gregory stared at him long and hard. At last he said, 'I believe you, though many wouldn't.' He stood up and moved out from behind the desk. 'Come here with me, and let me show you my collection.'

He led the way to the first of a row of glass-topped cases. 'All these things here are relics of the Roman occupation,' he said. 'Do you know about the Roman occupation?'

Jack shook his head. The case looked a bit like Nancy's stall. Inside it was a scattering of things that were not immediately recognisable but which looked as though they might be of some use to somebody. There were knives and spoons and buckles; strange coins with ugly faces on them, little figurines of bronze and white marble. In one corner there were fragments of broken crockery.

'You'll never fix that,' said Jack.

Gregory laughed. 'I'm sure you're right.' he said. 'Do you know how old these things are?'

'Pretty old,' said Jack. There was plenty of evidence of rust, but then there was on Nancy's stall as well.

'How high can you count?' asked Gregory.

Jack was proud of his counting. It was a new skill, one of the things that William had been teaching him, with great condescension.

'I can count nails in a horseshoe, sir,' he said. 'Six altogether, three on the inside and three on the outside, or sometimes eight if it's a very big shoe.'

'Ah,' said Gregory.

'And I can count farthings in a penny. And pennies in a shilling.'

'Very good. But not much more than that, eh?'

Jack shook his head. He knew that he was fourteen and

William was seventeen and his mother had been more than fifty. He knew that the year was 1720 as well, but he had no idea how it had got there.

'Well,' said Master Gregory. 'Let me think of another way of explaining how old these things are.' He paused for a moment and twisted his moustache, then went on. 'Think of your father, then think of your father's father, and his father before him, and then his father, and his father . . .'

Gregory went on, but he had lost Jack.

He was stuck fast at the first father; his own. He had been a sailor who spent most of his life aboard merchant ships which traded between England and Europe. Jack had rarely seen him, but when he did come home he infected the whole family with the passionate intensity of his life; the excitement and miseries of his work, the stories and shanties. He was a man of many moods, sometimes humorous and lively, sometimes withdrawn, sometimes explosive with rage and frustration. He never earned enough to relieve the constant hunger of his family or, if he did, he drank it. But he enriched their lives in other ways, bringing rare treats; fistfuls of sweet raisins and dates, strange little figures of people or animals, the occasional precious stone for his wife.

'. . . and his father, and his father . . .'

But there came a time when he didn't return. Perhaps someone told Jack that the ship had gone down in a storm, or perhaps he just decided it for himself. Since his mother's bitter comments about his father made no sense to him, he ignored them. But a year before, his one surviving sister Alice had told him the truth, just a few days before she entered into service for a merchant near Reading and disappeared from Jack's life forever. Their father wasn't in Davy Jones' Locker at all, but had taken a second wife in Portsmouth and was living there still. Since then, Jack had successfully avoided thinking about him. Until now.

'. . . his father, and his father again. When that man was a boy, Jack, Britain was occupied by the Romans. And that was when these things were made. Can you imagine how old they are?'

But Jack was wondering what kind of a man would abandon his family like that. Two of his sisters had died since then, too weak to withstand an attack of scarlet fever.

'More than fifteen hundred years old.'

Jack felt weak with grief and anger. He didn't care for himself, but little Jenny had bounced on his knee and smiled at him and tried out her first words . . . He should have gone to find him. He should have hounded him down, confronted him with the truth of what he had done. Perhaps he still could? Walk away from the mad collector and his useless, decaying treasures . . .

'Jack?'

'Yes, sir?'

'Do you see how old these things are?'

'Yes, sir.'

Gregory moved on to another case, similar to the first. Inside, all the pieces were made of stone.

'These things are even older. There's no way of knowing just how old they are, but they came from a time before mankind had discovered how to use metal.'

'Are they relics?'

'Yes, they are. Look.' Gregory opened the case and picked up a piece of glinting stone shaped a bit like a wood-cutter's wedge. 'If you take a piece of flint from the ground, it's not a relic, it's just a piece of flint. But if someone in the past has taken another piece of stone and shaped the flint into an axe-head like this one, that makes it a relic. A relic is something that someone has made.'

Jack nodded. 'Is my thing a relic?'

Gregory looked thoughtful for a moment, then said, 'Not exactly, no. But it is interesting.'

Jack had forgotten his father again. His heart was racing with hope. But Gregory clearly wasn't ready to discuss business yet. He took Jack around the entire room, pointing out swords and shields and spears, pieces of mouldering harness, gold and silver jewellery, pots and jugs, some whole, some broken. Several cases were filled with religious relics, and

Jack found himself listening to the history of Christianity in England.

Sometimes he was fascinated, and sometimes bored. He was longing to ask why Gregory wanted all those things, but he didn't dare in case he should think about it and decide that he didn't. When they finally finished the inspection, Jack was a little wiser but not much. None of the names or facts or figures had stayed with him; he didn't have that kind of mind. But he had learned two things. One was that everything in that room was old, and that old meant valuable. The other was that in the whole collection there was not a single item like his own. He could not, however, decide whether this was a good or a bad thing.

Master Gregory sat down at his desk. The rain had stopped and, through a gap in the clouds, the sun sent a pool of brilliance to show Jack's little pot in the best possible light. Since Gregory seemed reluctant to say anything, Jack felt compelled to open the negotiations.

'Do you know what it is?'

'Yes, I do,' said Gregory. 'It is perhaps most commonly known as a "philosopher's egg".'

Jack disliked big words and, as for eggs, he preferred not to think about them. His concern, in any case, was more immediate. 'Is it very old?' he said.

'No. It's not old at all.'

Jack's spirits sank. His mind, suddenly empty, conjured up an image of old Dobbs. His eyes were full of scorn, reminding Jack that he deserved no better.

'It's not valuable, then?'

'I don't know,' said Gregory. 'I just don't know.' He picked up the pot and shook it beside his ear as Nancy had done. A faint flush passed over his pale cheeks and he put it down again. Valuable or not, the object seemed to exert a kind of attraction over Gregory that made Jack's skin crawl. He remembered the farm boy and realised he was probably right. Gregory must be mad to spend his life indoors, surrounded by ancient, useless things.

Silence fell and stretched on. The sun withdrew behind the

clouds again. Jack noticed that his clothes were nearly dry. He pulled at a loose thread and rolled it into a ball. Then he picked his nose and scratched at the lice in his mop of dust-brown hair. Eventually Gregory straightened up in his chair.

'I need some time to think about this,' he said. 'It's not an easy decision.'

Jack nodded eagerly. Anything was better than a rejection.

'Do you mind waiting for a while?'

Jack was baffled by being asked. All his life he had been told where to go and what to do. He wasn't even sure of how to answer the question.

'Mrs Brown will take care of you in the meantime,' Gregory went on, 'and I will let you know as soon as I make up my mind.'

Chapter Six

Mrs Brown was evidently displeased by her additional duties. She took Jack to the washroom in the servants' quarters, handed him a bar of strong-smelling brown soap and refused to allow him out until he promised that he had scrubbed himself from head to toe. She ordered the maid to wash his clothes and gave him an old shirt of Master Gregory's to wear in the meantime. It fitted him like a night-gown, the tails hanging down to his ankles. Finally, he was permitted to come and sit quietly in the corner of the kitchen.

Mrs Brown carried on with her work and ignored him. The maid returned with his clothes and hung them on a rail above the hob, where they were soon steaming as heartily as the kettle. Outside the sky darkened and the rain began again, with angry thunder and lightning. Mrs Brown closed the shutters and sat in semi-darkness, running a string of beads through her fingers and muttering strange invocations. Jack wondered if the whole household might not be mad. He rocked and fidgeted on his stool and wished that Gregory would come to some decision. But the storm passed and Mrs Brown opened the shutters again, and still there was no word.

Supper was prepared; cold cuts of ham with fresh bread, butter and radishes. Mrs Brown prepared a tray and took it up to the master in his room. When she came down again she glared at Jack as though she was trying to melt him where he sat and then, begrudgingly, set a plate for him at the table.

'He says I'm to feed you. Sit up here.'

Jack sat up, looking with dismay at the knife and fork beside the plate. He had never used them before. But Mrs Brown didn't notice.

'I don't usually feed them,' she was saying. 'They just come with their bits of old rubbish and go away again. What is that thing that you came with, anyway?'

'I don't know,' said Jack.

'I don't suppose anybody else does, either. He's weak in the head, that one. He just sits up there brooding over all those bits and pieces. I'll never understand it.'

She ranted on, but Jack was falling upon the ham and heard no more. Here was meat, twice in one day, and he was determined to do it justice. When he had eaten all he could, he felt drowsy and curled up on the firewood box beside the hob. His clothes, he noticed, were nearly dry. In a minute or two he would get up and put them on.

When he woke, the dawn light was creeping in through the closed shutters. The fire was out, but the weather was still muggy and Jack hadn't suffered at all from sleeping without a blanket. He got up and went out into the yard and stood for a while, enchanted by the clamour of birdsong in the tall trees around the house. Then he went back into the kitchen, helped himself to a dipper of water from the cool crock in the scullery and dressed himself in his own clothes.

It was some time before Mrs Brown arrived, bleary-eyed and cross. She set to work immediately, clearing the ashes and setting a new fire. Jack seemed to be constantly in her way, and when he took refuge on a stool beside the table she hauled him off it and sent him out to the sheds for firewood. By the time he had filled the box, the fire was burning briskly and a pot of oatmeal was hissing on the hob.

Jack watched it, wishing it would boil. A boy came from the dairy with milk. Mrs Brown was just pouring some into a bowl for a pair of scrawny cats, when the loud clang of a call bell made her jump and slosh it on to the floor.

'Sorry,' said Jack, just for being there. Mrs Brown accepted his apology and strode off towards the hall, wiping her hands on her fresh, white apron.

A few moments later she was back. 'It's you he wants.'

Jack hesitated. The porridge was just beginning to bubble enticingly.

'Go on,' said Mrs Brown. 'Don't keep him waiting.'

He jumped down from the wood box and ran through the great, empty house. His bare feet made hardly any sound, as though he were so insubstantial that the heavy flagstones of the hall and the solid oak of the stairs could not even feel his presence. Up on the landing, Master Gregory's door was still ajar. Jack knocked lightly.

'Come in.'

Despite its great size, the room was stuffy. There was a faint hint of decay, as though some small creature had perished beneath the floorboards and was slowly rotting there. To Jack's relief, his pot was still on the desk where he had last seen it. Mr Gregory was standing above it, swaying slightly.

'Has Mrs Brown been taking care of you?' he asked.

'Yes, sir.'

'Did you sleep well?'

'Very well.'

'That's good. I'm afraid that I didn't sleep at all.'

'Are you ill?' Jack asked.

Gregory certainly looked ill. His moustache seemed to droop more than ever and a pale haze of stubble covered his jaw. His eyes were listless, and beneath them the darkness was deeper than ever. But he shook his head and smiled, wistfully.

'Your little offering here has been causing me a great deal of dismay.'

His words gave the object an air of malevolence that Jack had not noticed before. 'Shall I take it away?' he said.

'Probably, yes,' said Gregory. 'But first I want to tell you what I know about it and then we can decide what to do.' He gestured to a small upholstered stool beneath the desk. Jack took it out and sat on it. Outside, the rain clouds had vanished completely and the morning sun was blazing through the tall windows. Jack squinted and turned his back to it. Master Gregory cleared his throat.

'I have not turned out as my father would have wished,' he said.

Jack squirmed. When his mother had been alive, she had

sometimes cornered him on dark evenings beside the fire and subjected him to long, mournful diatribes about her wasted life. That kind of adult intimacy embarrassed him. He turned away pointedly, but Gregory did not notice.

'I never married, never provided him with a grandson to continue the family line. Most of my estate is let to my neighbours,' he went on. 'I do not manage any of it. I do not keep a pack of hounds as he did. I rarely even ride. I don't know why it is, but my only interest in life is my collection. My father died a disappointed man.'

Jack gazed out of the window. Gregory was quiet for a minute, and at last Jack felt compelled to look at him again.

'Am I boring you?' he asked.

'No.'

Gregory sighed. 'I'm only telling you this because I want you to know that I have had plenty of opportunity in my life to search my soul. But I have never searched it more deeply than I did last night, sitting here with this . . .' his eyes fell on the pot and his voice trailed off.

Jack looked at the plain little thing and wondered how it could possibly be the cause of so much mystery. He thought of Mrs Brown's porridge, which would surely be cooked by now. But Master Gregory clearly wasn't ready for breakfast, yet.

'Do you know what an alchemist is, Jack?' he said.

'No, sir.'

'Well, this thing here was made by one.'

'What for?'

'For the practice of his art. Alchemy.'

More strange words. They made Jack feel tired. He was fast running out of curiosity about the philosopher's egg and was beginning to wish that he had never set eyes upon it. But Gregory's next words changed his mind again.

'The alchemists believe that they can make gold, Jack. In just such a vessel as this.'

A flush of excitement quickened Jack's heart. Gold. The answer to all life's problems. The reward at the end of the rainbow. The fairy-tale promise of happiness. 'And can they?'

Gregory shrugged. 'No one really knows. Alchemy is a dark art, they say. The king does not approve of it, and the alchemists keep themselves and their work well hidden. Their writings are obscure and secretive, a sort of code among themselves. But I believe I know where this one comes from. What perplexes me, though, is how it came to be in the river.'

Jack couldn't care less. His mind was running along more practical lines. 'Can we make some gold with it?' he asked.

Gregory laughed, a melancholy sort of sound which gave Jack the shivers. 'I wish it were so simple,' he said.

'Why isn't it?'

'To begin with, we don't know what to put in it. And aside from that . . .' he hesitated and peered at Jack with a searching expression as though wondering whether or not he could be trusted. Then he sighed as if he were relinquishing something. 'Aside from that,' he went on, 'it's possible, just possible, that it has already been done.'

For a moment or two Jack had no idea what Gregory was talking about. Then, slowly, it dawned on him. 'You mean there might be gold in it already?'

'It's unlikely, but it's possible, yes.'

'Then let's open it!'

But Gregory shook his head sadly.

'That is precisely the dilemma that has kept me from my bed throughout the night,' he said. 'I could have done it, you see? I could have broken it the instant you went out of the door last night. If there was gold inside I could have kept it for myself and sent you off with a penny for your trouble. You would never have known.'

'But that wouldn't have been right!'

'Of course it wouldn't. And I'm glad to say that I didn't do it for just that reason.' Gregory sighed again. 'And in any case, what use have I for gold? I have no wife or family and my father left more than enough behind him to keep me and my collection going until the end of my life. But even so, curiosity alone might have compelled me to break it. If my conscience disturbed me I could have given the gold to you.'

Jack nodded eagerly. 'Shall we do it now, then?'

'It's not so simple, don't you see?'

'Why?'

'Many reasons. For one thing, the god-fearing side of my nature keeps prompting me to have nothing to do with this devilish practice. It is far better left alone.'

'I can do it, then,' said Jack. 'I'm not scared.'

'Ah, but there's another reason for not opening it, Jack. A much better one.'

'Is there?'

Gregory nodded solemnly. 'What if there is no gold inside it? What then?'

Jack shook his head in bewilderment. His spirits were being dragged this way and that, like a rat between two terriers.

'What if nothing came out except a mess of noxious chemicals? It's quite possible, you know. Many of society's greatest thinkers have said that alchemy is preposterous, practised only by lunatics. They say that there are no powers known to man that can turn base metals into gold. What if they are right?'

Jack had no answer. Gregory supplied it for him. 'Then we are left with a broken pot, without the slightest value to either of us.'

For a moment neither of them spoke. Then Jack marshalled the thoughts that were circling his mind like buzzards. 'But what if we don't break it? What value does it have to us then?'

'None.'

He was definitely mad. There was no doubt in Jack's mind whatsoever. The sooner he got out of that house the better. He stood up and edged his way up to the desk, but as he reached out to take the alchemist's vessel, Gregory laid a hand on his arm.

'It has no value to you or I, Jack,' he said, 'but it may be of value to someone else.'

'Who?'

'The alchemist who made it. And I believe I know who he is.' He picked up the vessel and held it between them. 'I don't know exactly what kind of material it's made from, but I can tell that it has been subjected to intense heat. In other words, whatever is inside it has been cooked. Do you see?'

Jack shook his head.

'Well,' Gregory went on. 'It has been cooked but it hasn't been opened. So no one, not even the alchemist himself can possibly know whether the experiment has been successful.'

'You mean he doesn't know if there's gold in it or not?'

'Exactly.'

'Then why don't we open it and see?'

Gregory gasped in exasperation. 'Listen carefully, Jack. If we open it and find nothing, then I have nothing, you have nothing and the alchemist has nothing, not even his vessel. But if you take it to the alchemist he is sure to give you something for your trouble, isn't he? He may even reward you well. He may be desperate to find it again.'

'But what if there is gold in it?' said Jack, feeling fairly desperate himself.

'Then we will all have what we are looking for. The alchemist will have his gold. You will have the few coppers that you hoped to get from me.'

Jack nodded. It seemed that there was some sense in what Gregory was saying, after all.

'But what about you?' he said. 'You will have nothing.'

'Not so, dear Jack. I have the pleasure of a rare victory of conscience. For once in my life I will have done the right thing. And that is worth more to me than any amount of gold.'

Chapter Seven

THE name of the alchemist was Jonathan Barnstable. His house was beside the river, further inland again, and Mr Gregory gave Jack careful directions, making him repeat them over and over again until they were perfectly fixed in his mind. On this occasion, there was no question of asking the way. Nor must Jack reveal the nature of that which he carried, no matter what pressure might be brought to bear. Gregory provided him with the cut-off corner of a flour sack in which to conceal the philosopher's egg and Mrs Brown, despite her continued sourness, added a good cut of ham between two slices of bread.

So Jack set off again along more new roads, into more uncertainty. The sun shone from a clear sky on to trees and hedgerows where birds dislodged the last hanging drops of rain to fall sparkling among the leaves. As the day warmed up, steam began to rise from the damp ground, releasing the sweet scents of worm-turned earth and sprouting seeds. Already the stubble in the raked over meadows seemed greener than it had the day before.

According to Master Gregory, it was eight miles from Dulwich to the small town where the alchemist lived. At a brisk walk, he had said, Jack could cover that distance in two or three hours. But it wasn't a day for walking briskly. It was a day for dawdling and soaking up the sun. It was a day for picking wild raspberries and smelling briar roses and tossing pebbles into streams. Even the farmers who had failed to save their hay were in no hurry as they worked their way across their meadows, shaking out the sodden rows to dry all over again. After two hours, Jack was less than halfway there. His stomach was empty and the bread and ham was beginning to exert a strong influence. He began to look out for a good spot to stop and take a rest.

Before long he found it. A cart track crossed the road and at the corner of it a huge horse-chestnut tree created a secretive sort of den with its lowest branches. Jack looked around to be sure there was no one watching, then crept inside, making his way carefully around behind the huge old trunk until he was sure that he could not be seen from the road. Between the roots were dusty hollows which the rain had not reached; armchairs for idling children or tired travellers. As Jack settled himself in a fat pigeon took flight, clattering through the branches and producing a gentle shower of leaves and feathers. After that, there was silence.

Jack took his time over the meal, prolonging the enjoyment. When he had finished he lay back against the trunk of the tree and gazed up into the branches, where light and shade intertwined like lovers. Gradually he slipped into a brief sleep, and when he woke he could not remember where he was and what he was doing there. He sat up and his eye fell on the pot lying in the open sack. It all came back to him then, except the conviction in what he was doing. The more he thought about it, the more uncertain he became. He wasn't at all sure that he wanted to meet any alchemist. What kind of a man would he be? Why should the whole business be so secretive?

Perhaps it was because there really was gold. Jack took the pot out of the sack and laid it with great care on a level piece of ground. Then he searched around among the roots until he found a stone heavy enough to break it. The surrounding countryside was quite silent. Jack raised the stone above his head, imagining the pot cracking like an eggshell and a smooth, shining yolk of gold rolling out. But before he could make the crucial blow, Gregory's words came back to him.

'What if nothing came out except a mess of noxious chemicals?'

Jack froze where he stood as a dreadful image came into his mind. He had been at home, years ago, watching his mother kneeling beside the hearth. Behind her, hunched in the chimney corner, his brother Matty was dying of consumption.

'I have an egg for you, Matty,' his mother said. 'This will build up your strength again now, won't it?'

Matty looked out with hollow, hopeless eyes. His mother held the egg out for him to see, then cracked it on the edge of the hot pan. But instead of white and yellow, a thin, green sludge came out. As it hit the pan a foul stench rose up and made Jack retch until his ribs hurt.

That night, Matty died. Jack had been too young to realise that he would have died anyway, and he believed that if the egg had not been rotten, his brother would have lived. The incident convinced him that some sort of celestial cruelty existed; some dreadful corruption at the heart of things. The image remained with him for years, creeping into his mind in the minutes before sleep and invading his dreams. At the bleakest times of his life it returned to torment him, sticking in his mind with a terrible tenacity that he could not defeat. At his mother's graveside he could not tell whether the smell that surrounded him had risen from the dark earth or from the memory of that rotten egg.

He looked down at the pot, and knew that he couldn't break it. As long as it was still intact then hope was, too. He drew back his arm and flung the stone as high as he could into the branches above him, filling the air with frightened birds and swirling leaves. Then he wrapped the pot back up in its sack and rejoined the road.

It was market day and the small town was teeming with life. Jack was tempted to stay and watch, just for the familiarity of being surrounded by people, but Gregory's warnings had made him aware of the danger of discovery and he passed on through. As he left the town, the sky clouded over again and the air cooled down. There would soon be more rain.

The alchemist lived half a mile outside the town, at the end of a narrow, green track which looked as though it were rarely used. Any doubts that Jack might have had were dispelled when he saw the garden. It was, as Master Gregory had told him, the finest garden that Jack was ever likely to see. On one side of the flagged path which led up to the front door a forest of vegetables was growing. Carrot tops crowded each other for space like rows of bracken beside huge, perfectly formed cabbages. Enormous marrows, ripe to bursting, lay beneath the shade of their bushes. Red beetroot tops grew between rows of spinach and parsnips and the whole area was fenced in by ranks of tall onions.

Jack was just about to open the little wicket gate when something caused him to stop. On the other side of the path was the orchard, where a dozen or so chickens and a cock wandered and scratched. Beneath one of the trees the figure of a man was stooping down, as though picking something up from the ground. Jack waited for him to straighten up, but he didn't move, not an inch. As he watched, Jack noticed another figure; a woman in a sack-cloth dress, stretching up towards a cherry tree laden with ripe fruit. She wasn't moving, either, though her skirts swayed in the light breeze. Suddenly Jack realised that there were people everywhere, merging in among the shadows of the orchard. A chill tingled his spine. They were all frozen, locked into one position or another beneath the ripening apples and plums. Perhaps they had been caught stealing fruit? Jack had heard of such things in fairy tales. If the alchemist could make gold, he could surely turn people into stone as well.

Jack was about to take to his heels when he noticed a cat in the branches of the cherry tree above the woman's head. As the tree shifted in the breeze, he could see quite clearly that the cat wasn't made of stone at all, but of straw. He let out a long-held breath. They were all scarecrows. Weird and wonderful scarecrows. And it appeared as if they worked. A few wasps buzzed in and out of the shadows, but there were no birds to be seen among the trees at all. The lush crop of cherries was the proof. Jack lifted the latch of the gate and walked through it on to the onion-scented path.

He stood there for a while, looking ahead at the old house. The walls were of rough stone, smoothed and softened by successive coats of lime. Ivy and honeysuckle climbed with the same luxuriant growth as the vegetables and made their own frames for the door and windows, so that there seemed to be no corners or angles anywhere. The roof-line dipped and swayed where the green timbers that had been used to build it had warped and made themselves comfortable, and the thatch which covered them was shaggy as Dobbs' winter coat. Indeed, the house seemed more like a living creature than a building, but it was a friendly one, and Jack felt quite comfortable as he began to walk forward again. He examined the scarecrows as he passed. None of them had faces, and now that he knew what they were, they did not seem forbidding at all. But when one of them detached itself from the shadows and began to walk towards him, Jack nearly lost his grip on the pot.

'Good afternoon to you.'

The man was wearing a collarless shirt like Jack's with leather braces, moleskin trousers and a pair of large, dusty boots. Although his hair was almost white he looked as strong as a horse, his square hands roughened by work, his face and arms darkened by long hours in the sun.

'Lost your tongue, lad?'

He was one of the tallest men that Jack had ever seen, but it was not his height that struck Jack speechless. It was the bright blue eyes, which shone with a youthful, almost childlike light.

'I see you have.'

Jack craned his neck to look up into the man's face. 'Are you here working?' he said.

The blue eyes took on a mischievous glint. 'As you can see,' he said.

'For Mr Barnstable, I meant.'

'I would work for no one else,' said the man, 'since I am Mr Barnstable.'

'Oh.' Jack was disappointed. He wasn't sure what he had expected, but it hadn't been someone who looked like a labourer. If a man could make gold, surely there would be some evidence of it? Fine clothes at least, and servants. He didn't know what to say so he said nothing. Barnstable said nothing either, but retreated into the shadows of the orchard. Jack watched a thrush hopping among the radishes and tried to remember why he had come.

'Oh!' he called. 'I have something here belonging to you.'

Barnstable re-emerged, his hands full of cherries. 'Have you?' he said.

'Yes.' Jack held up the piece of sacking. 'Or at least, Master Gregory thinks so.'

'Does he indeed. Well, perhaps he's right.' He smiled at Jack. 'Will you swop it for these?'

Without a second thought, Jack held out the sack and accepted the rich, red cherries. There were more than he could fit in his cupped hands, and they spilled out on to the path at his feet. He sat down and began to eat them. Nothing had ever tasted sweeter.

Barnstable untied the sack and gave a surprised laugh. 'So you came back to me,' he said.

Jack looked at him quizzically.

'Not you,' said the alchemist. 'This. My sacred vessel.'

'It is yours, then?'

'Yes, it is, Billy. It is. I never expected to see it again.'

'Who's Billy?' said Jack.

'Why, you are, aren't you?'

'No. I'm Jack.'

Barnstable looked at him closely. 'Are you sure?'

'Yes. I'm quite sure.'

The mischievous glint had returned to Barnstable's eyes. 'How strange,' he said.

At that moment the clouds burst and rain began to pour out of the skies. The thrush hopped up from among the radishes and soared away over Jack's head to some tall poplars beyond the orchard. The chickens began to make for the shelter of a lean-to at the side of the house. Barnstable ran up the path and sprang on to the doorstep with surprising agility.

'Come on,' he called.

Jack gathered up the remaining cherries and raced up to the house. As he followed the alchemist through the low doorway he had a brief sensation of walking into a cluster of undergrowth: the inside of the house was as much alive as the outside. Plants grew everywhere, out of buckets and pots and crocks and cut-down barrels. Ivy wandered up the walls and wound around the ladder which led to the loft. In a crack in the front windowsill, a sycamore seedling had taken root. The alchemist watched Jack's reaction and smiled. Then he led the way on through a muddle of tools and boxes to the back of the house.

Jack followed slowly, gazing around him. His eyes were becoming accustomed to the interior gloom and there were things everywhere that he wanted to see. There were shelves lined with books, their spines turned towards him, their secret hearts hidden. There was a pile of stones which glinted with different colours; reds and silvers and iridescent greens. The walls were hung with pictures; not grand portraits like the ones in Master Gregory's house but delicate drawings of kings and queens, of snakes which ate their own tails, of vessels like the one he had just handed back to the alchemist. The house was saturated in mystery, but it didn't make Jack afraid. It thrilled him to the marrow.

Barnstable was in a cosy little room beside the scullery, looking out through the window. Jack went over and stood beside him. Behind the house the bank of the river sloped steeply down to the water's edge. With a hook and line, Jack could have tried for a fish without moving from where he stood. The surface of the water was pitted by the heavy rain.

'Good for my garden,' said the alchemist. There was a gentle smile on his face as he looked across the river, as though the rain had come as a special favour to him and he appreciated it. Suddenly, and with a painful intensity, Jack wanted Barnstable to look that way at him. He couldn't explain it, not even to himself, but there was somehow more to the alchemist than to anyone he had ever met. There was more gentleness, more humour, more kindness, more life. He wanted to stay there and be with him, to learn the secrets of the garden and the books and the pictures, to eat cherries and stand in simple silence at the window, looking out at the rain.

When the alchemist finally spoke, it was as if a spell had been broken.

'Where did you find the vessel, Billy?'

'In the river. And I'm not Billy, I'm Jack.'

'Yes, so you said. I find that very strange.'

'Why?'

Barnstable turned away from the window and leant against the sill. 'Because I thought all boys were called Billy. They are around here, anyway.' He began to count along his fingers. 'There's Billy Hobbs and Billy Miller and Billy Grace, then there's the three Billy Bakers, Billy Fisher. Oh, who else? Little Billy, One-eyed Billy, Billy the Boots and Pig Billy. I could go on and on. The town is full of Billys. But I never heard of a Jack.'

'Well, you have now,' said Jack. 'Where I come from all the boys have different names. There's Thomas and John and Robert and Oliver and . . .' he faltered, trying to remember.

'You're not going to tell me the girls have different names as well, are you?'

'Of course they do!' Jack moved round to face the alchemist and looked up into the brilliant blue eyes. 'There's Polly and Lizzie and Alice and Jenny. And lots more, too.'

Barnstable shook his head in puzzlement. 'If you weren't so earnest, Jack, I would have trouble believing you. The world is a strange place, isn't it?'

The way he said it reminded Jack of the mystery which surrounded him. The sense of excitement returned. 'Yes,' he said. 'It is.'

Barnstable moved away from the window and sat down in a chair beside the unlit hearth. He gestured towards a second chair and said, 'But you were telling me about finding the vessel. Do go on.'

Jack sat down on the edge of the chair. 'It was in the river, beside the old monastery. It was just in the water.'

'And what were you doing there?'

'I was just walking along.'

There was a silence. Jack looked at his feet and then, reluctantly, up into the calm gaze of the alchemist. There were no lies there, nor even the possibility of them. With a sense of shame, Jack began again.

'I was an apprentice to a blacksmith.'

He told the whole story, leaving nothing out, not even the

way he felt about Dobbs. It was strange to be saying it, as though it were a tale belonging to someone else, but the alchemist listened intently and gave gentle encouragement when Jack stumbled over a word or lost track of his thoughts. When he arrived at finding the pot he would have stopped, but Barnstable asked him to go on and tell everything, right up to his arrival at the gate. So Jack told him about the beggar and about Nancy and the journey to Master Gregory's house. He made a joke about the cases full of rubbish that Gregory kept, and was delighted when the alchemist laughed. What he didn't tell, because he didn't dare, was how close both he and Gregory had come to breaking open the precious vessel.

When he had said all he could think of to say, Jack waited expectantly. Barnstable stared at the hearth for a while, as though pondering on something, then sighed deeply.

'That Gregory is a strange one all right,' he said. 'I think we are safe enough, though. If he wished me harm he could have given me away a long time ago.'

'Given you away?'

'To those who govern the land, Jack. Alchemy has been outlawed for a long time now.'

'But why?'

Barnstable sighed again. 'Did Master Gregory tell you what an alchemist is?' he said.

'Yes, he did.'

'What did he tell you?'

'That they . . . that you make gold.'

'Yes.' Barnstable nodded. 'And if someone could make gold, they might turn out to be rich and powerful, mightn't they?'

'I suppose they might, yes.'

'As powerful as the king, perhaps?'

As the alchemist was speaking his tone become hushed and conspiratorial. His eyes shone with a fierce light, and Jack could imagine nothing more powerful on earth than what he saw in them. But before he could catch it, it was gone, replaced by humour again and kindness.

'Do you believe it, Jack?'

'Believe what?'

'That alchemists make gold?'

Jack didn't hesitate. 'Yes,' he said.

'Why?' said Barnstable. 'Why do you believe it?'

'Because Master Gregory told me so.'

'Then you believe everything that your elders tell you?'

Jack thought hard. He wasn't sure whether he did or he didn't.

'Do you believe, for instance,' Barnstable went on, 'that all the boys in this parish are called Billy?'

A red blush crept into Jack's cheeks. 'I did, sir, because you told me so.'

'And do you believe that alchemists can make gold?'

Jack's mind got stuck. The honesty that had compelled him to tell the truth seemed to have vanished from Barnstable's eyes. They were vacant now, revealing nothing, hard and clear as ice.

'Do you or don't you?'

The alchemist stood up and held the pot above his head, high over the stone floor. Still Jack couldn't answer. He had wanted to know for so long that he could hardly bear it, but still the thought of the precious vessel smashing into pieces on the floor filled him with terror.

'Well?'

It could all have been over, then; the truth revealed on the hard flagstones of Barnstable's floor. But Jack's hopes might have smashed along with the vessel. The smell of rotten eggs began to invade his mind.

'Do you believe there is gold in it, Jack?'

For one more moment Barnstable held the pot above the ground. Jack watched as his fingers relaxed their grip, and let go.

'Yes!' he yelled, at the top of his voice, and at the same instant the alchemist, with astonishing agility, plucked the falling vessel from the air with his left hand, just inches above the ground. He smiled delightedly at Jack, as child-like as ever. 'So do I,' he said.

Jack dropped his head between his knees and retched. Barnstable knelt beside him and laid a gentle hand on his shoulder.

'Here,' he said, putting the vessel on the ground between Jack's feet. 'It's yours. I'm giving it to you.'

Jack shook his head and pushed it away with a trembling hand. It was too late for that now. He knew that even if it was his, even if he believed, as he had said, that it was full of gold, he could never, never bring himself to make that final gesture and break it. The thing was useless; worthless. If he took it, it would burden his soul for the rest of his life.

'You don't want it?' said Barnstable.

'No!' Jack was surprised by his own certainty. 'I'm sick of the sight of it. I never want to see it again.'

The alchemist regarded him with a bemused smile. 'Won't take it, eh? Then what can I offer you instead? More cherries?'

Jack looked interested, but Barnstable shook his head. 'Cherries come and cherries go. They have a short season. But a man needs a trade, and any trade needs an apprenticeship, doesn't it? Can you go back to your blacksmith?'

Jack shuddered and shook his head.

'Then you need another apprenticeship, don't you? Since you won't accept the finished work that I offered you, how would you like to learn how to do it yourself?'

'Learn alchemy?' said Jack.

'Yes. I'll take you on as my apprentice. You can learn how to make gold for yourself.'

Chapter Eight

THERE were no indentures to be signed upon Jack's acceptance of his new apprenticeship, nor any agreement about the length of time to be served. The only formality was that Jack swore himself to absolute silence with regard to the secret art. Neither the practice of alchemy, nor anything connected with it was ever to be mentioned to anyone, no matter what the circumstances.

When that was over, Barnstable sent Jack to the scullery for a bowl of water while he went out to the garden. He returned shortly with a carrot, a parsnip and a pair of green onions. The carrot was as long as Jack's forearm, and the parsnip rather longer. The bruised stems of the onions filled the air with their scent. Barnstable brought a knife and a chopping board from the scullery and set them on the floor beside the bowl of water.

'The art of alchemy,' he said, 'is not so very different from cooking. To begin with, it makes use of the same elements. The first one is earth, represented by these.' He picked up the vegetables and handed them to Jack. 'The next is water, in which you may now wash them and in which we will later cook them. The third is air, which we will trap between the water and the lid of the pot, compelling it to swirl around as vapour and accelerate the process. But none of this can happen without the fourth element, can it?'

He paused, and Jack had the uncomfortable feeling that he was expected to say something. He hadn't been listening very closely to what the alchemist was saying, partly because the big words made him feel sleepy and partly because the sight of those magnificent vegetables had made him feel extremely hungry.

'What else do we need, Jack, before we can cook our meal?'

Jack searched through his mind but found it so full of strange new images and concepts that he wasn't sure he knew his way around it any more.

'Salt?' he said, at last.

Barnstable smiled gently. 'Salt is a useful ingredient, yes,' he said. 'But even salt won't cook our supper for us. Only fire will do that.'

He proceeded to light one in the wide fireplace while Jack, embarrassed by his own stupidity, tried to make up for it by washing the vegetables and chopping them into neat pieces. Soon the flames were crackling up through the kindling, making the room feel cosy, despite the rain rattling against the window behind them. Barnstable threw a handful of barley and peas on top of the vegetables in the pot, added water and salt, and sealed them all in beneath the heavy lid. Jack hefted it up on to the sooty hook which hung above the hearth and for a while they both sat in the afternoon gloom and watched the fire take hold. The alchemist's face was soft and kind beneath his silvering hair and Jack, for the first time in his life, felt welcome and safe.

The river slapped and sloshed against its banks. The wind gusted at the chimney, causing the fire to wuffle and roar, then collapse into quiescence again. Gradually the pot began to hum, then to hiss, and finally to bubble.

Barnstable sighed, and Jack heard his bones crackle like the kindling as he stretched himself out and then recoiled again. He stood up, walked over to the fireside and, with exaggerated care, added two more logs.

'The fire cannot be treated with too much respect,' he said. 'That is your second lesson on the alchemical process.'

Jack nodded gravely, hoping to conceal the fact that he had no recollection whatsoever of any first lesson.

'The world is full of puffers,' Barnstable went on. 'Men and women who make the mistake of trying to speed up a process which must take place in its own good time. They fan the flames, like this.' He picked up a pair of bellows which leant against the wall and aimed them at the fire. 'Puff, puff, puff, you see? That's why we call them puffers.'

Jack watched as the fire began to glow angrily at the centre, then send flames leaping around the black pot. He wondered whether he should confess, explain about the bellows in the forge and how he was a puffer already. Perhaps there was a cure for it?

The alchemist laid the bellows down. 'And what happens if the fire is too hot?' he asked.

'The fuel gets wasted?' The only time that the fire in the forge was ever too hot was when there was no work to be done. The usual problem was that it wasn't hot enough.

Barnstable nodded, thoughtfully. 'That's true, I suppose. But I was thinking more of what happens to the pottage.'

'It gets burned?'

'Exactly. Our meal is ruined. But when we are dealing with the volatile elements in our other sort of cookery, the alchemical sort, the results can be far worse. I have heard of puffers, Jack, who exploded themselves and their workshops in their desperate hurry to get rich. Fools. Even if they hadn't, they would not have succeeded. Their experiments would never have worked.' He walked over to a box in the corner of the fireplace. 'Come and look at this.'

Jack joined him. He had assumed that the box was for firewood, but now he noticed that the top was drilled with round holes. The alchemist lifted the lid. Inside was a hen, her feathers fluffed up for brooding and spread wide over her clutch of eggs. She gave Jack a hard stare and crooned a warning at him. Barnstable chuckled fondly and carefully closed the lid again.

'The great work is just like that,' he said. 'Like a hen hatching an egg. Too much or too little heat will kill the life within. The temperature must remain constant, and for that, the fire must be closely attended. This requires great patience. The philosopher who has no patience will not acquire the stone. Alchemy is simple, Jack, but it is not easy. Do you understand what I mean by that?'

'Not really,' said Jack.

'Good. You will, given time. Let's take a look at the laboratory, shall we?'

Beneath the pot, the flames had returned to their former size. The fire burned sweetly on.

*

Jack followed the alchemist through the scullery and into the workshop which lay beyond. As the door closed behind him, the mystery that he had sensed in the house seemed to fold in around him like a dense mist. The room was rectangular, the long walls twice the length of the short ones, and everywhere he looked there were pictures. There were snakes and dragons and blue eagles, there were lions and warriors, suns, moons and stars. The Red King and the White Queen were represented several times, in different forms, and it seemed to Jack that everywhere he looked they were gazing down at him from the walls. He stayed near the door and scrutinized them all surreptitiously.

One of the pictures in particular caught Jack's attention. In most of them, the royal pair were odd-looking caricatures, but in this one they were so realistic that they gave Jack the impression of being real people, standing in the room. They were young, and they stood an arm's length apart, turning slightly towards each other. The queen was standing on a globe, her hair tucked up beneath her crown; her long, white gown hanging in elegant folds from her shoulders. The king stood in a small bonfire, which licked around his feet, yet he seemed to be in no discomfort. He was handsome and, Jack decided, infinitely strong and brave.

Barnstable returned to Jack's side and stood with him, regarding the royal pair. 'You like them?' he said.

Jack nodded. He did like them. They captured his imagination in a way no other pictures ever had.

'The Red King and the White Queen,' said Barnstable. Red sulphur and white lead.'

'Uh?' said Jack.

'The two most crucial elements in the alchemical mixture. Without them there is no beginning, and with no beginning, how can there be an end?'

Jack knew about sulphur and lead. He had come across them both at various times in London's markets. 'What's an element?' he said. 'They look like people to me.'

'Hmm,' said the alchemist. 'These are difficult areas, Jack, and not easy to understand. Elements are easy enough to explain, but in time you will come to see that the business of making gold isn't confined to what happens inside the philosopher's egg. It's about something that takes place inside the philosopher as well.'

The words made no sense to Jack, and, as he usually did on such occasions, he chose to ignore them. He turned his attention to another picture. In this one the king and queen were standing on either side of a small, radiant child, with a winged helmet and a staff with a snake wound around it.

'The divine child,' said Barnstable. 'The result of their union. The desired end of all our efforts.'

Jack drew his eyes from the picture. 'I thought the desired end was gold?'

'Of course,' said the alchemist. 'But which matters more? Gold in the hand or gold in the spirit?'

It was not a matter which had ever troubled Jack. If gold in the hand was an option, any alternative was of no consequence. His response to the question was to move away from the door and begin to look around the workshop.

In the centre of it was a long range of brick ovens and hobs. Jack had somehow formed the impression that the process of making gold never stopped, and he was disappointed to find that not a single fire was burning. A fine film of ash and dust covered the cold surface, as though it were some time since the workshop had been used.

'I no longer practice the art,' said the alchemist, 'though it is not so long since I did.'

'Why?' said Jack.

'Because I no longer need to.'

'You have enough gold?'

'More than enough.'

Jack looked around hopefully but there was still no evidence of it. Against one wall stood a row of high tables covered with bottles and jars and jugs, boxes and canisters, vessels of all shapes and sizes. There was an acrid smell that reminded Jack uncomfortably of his rotten egg, and he wondered if it was the result of experiments gone wrong.

Barnstable was standing beside the window which, like the

one in the room they had just left, looked out over the river. At the opposite end, a heavy curtain covered what Jack took to be another window, looking out to the front.

'Is this so that people can't see in?' he asked.

'No,' said the alchemist. 'There was a window there once, but it has long since been blocked up.' He walked the length of the room and drew the curtain aside.

Jack stepped backwards until he collided with the end of the range and was made to stop. Beneath the curtain was a picture which filled him at once with fear and exhilaration. It was of a man though he was, like the alchemist himself, much more than a man. There were wings on his heels and on the silver helmet that he wore. In one hand he held a sword with flames coming out of its tip, and in the other a staff around which two snakes intertwined. At his feet a third snake lay in a circle, its tail in its mouth. Beneath him were the Red King and the White Queen, kneeling.

'This is he who watches over the great work,' said the alchemist. 'Without him there is no hope of success. He is the highest and the lowest, the master of all ingenuity and inspiration. He is everywhere.'

'But . . . who is he?'

'He has many names. Hermes, Mercurius, Mercury. He is the lord of the secret art, the seal of our crucibles, the spirit in matter. There are many who call our learning the hermetic philosophy because of his rulership over it. Without Hermes, there is no alchemy. It is as simple as that.' He stepped back and drew the curtain again. '*Solvite corpora et coagulate spiritum*,' he said. 'Do you know Latin, Jack?'

Jack shook his head. 'Do I need to?' He was beginning to sense that the whole business was way beyond him. Part of him was already wishing that Barnstable would realise how unsuitable he was and throw him back out into the relative safety of the rain.

'Some time, perhaps. But not now. What I said was "Dissolve the body and coagulate the spirit". It means to make the body liquid and the spirit solid.' The alchemist saw Jack's confusion and laughed. 'Don't worry,' he said. 'There are plenty of things that you can't be expected to understand just yet. There's no hurry. Take your time. Don't be a puffer. Always remember that patience is the ladder of the philosophers.'

Jack discovered that he was required to exercise it immediately. The river slopped against its banks and the rain stopped, started, and stopped again while the alchemist explained every single feature of the workshop. He showed Jack the different kinds of vessels; alembics for purifying chemicals, pelicans with many-layered caps for distillations, crucibles for the heavier work of smelting ores and precious metals. He showed him some of the ingredients used in the great work; red sulphur with the rotten egg smell, white magnesia which he called the 'salt in the pottage', and finally, he showed him brilliant mercury itself, quicksilver, a metal that looked like silver but behaved like water.

'This one is the master of them all, Jack,' he said, pouring a small sample from a phial on to a marble work-bench where it scattered into small balls and skittered about.

'Can you catch him, Jack? Can you pick him up and hold him in your hand?'

Jack reached for one of the larger balls of quicksilver, but when he touched it, it broke into smaller ones which slithered away from his fingers. For a while he chased them fruitlessly, until eventually he managed to brush one from the edge of the bench on to the palm of his hand.

The alchemist looked delighted. 'Well done, well done. There he is, sitting on your hand like a butterfly. But how will you hold on to him, eh? In case he slips away again?'

Jack closed his fist around the silvery bead and watched helplessly as it broke into tiny droplets which squeezed between his fingers and fell to the floor. Barnstable laughed, gleefully.

'That is his nature, Jack. Don't ever forget it.'

They moved on around the workshop and discussed the different fireboxes in the range; open ones for direct heat, contained ones for fusion, and the great athanor, the oven within an oven where the philosopher's egg could be kept at an ever-constant temperature. Finally, when Jack feared that his patience was about to run out, the alchemist showed him a vessel just like the one that he had found in the river. The only difference was that this one was empty. Its neck had not been sealed.

'Would you like this one to be yours, Jack?'

'Mine?'

'Yours.'

'To make gold in?'

The alchemist nodded, but Jack could see a twinkle in his eye that he was beginning to recognise. The realisation came to him that since he had first found the pot floating in the river his life had consisted of rising hopes that proceeded to get dashed. He looked up at the curtain which hung over the picture of Hermes on the wall. He could feel his presence like dampness in the air.

'But it's not that simple, is it?'

The alchemist roared with laughter. 'I knew I wasn't wrong,' he said. 'You felt him, Jack, didn't you? You listened and you heard him, right here in this room. I'll make an alchemist of you, yet!'

Jack felt himself lifted on the crest of Barnstable's delight. 'Will you?' he said.

'Of course! And what's more, lad, the vessel is yours. It is as simple as that.'

Jack forgot about Hermes. 'Is it?'

'It is.' Barnstable opened the workshop door and ushered Jack through ahead of him. Then, as he closed it again behind them both, he said, 'But it might not be as easy as you think.'

It took Jack's appetite away. The fire was still burning gently beneath the pot and the little room was fuggy with rich steam from the pottage. Outside the misted window the birds were celebrating the end of the rain, but Jack's heart was hollow. He was tired, and not at all sure that he wanted to continue with this apprenticeship.

The alchemist took the lid from the pot and made all kinds

of appreciative noises, then filled two bowls to the brim. As soon as he began to eat, Jack's appetite returned and neither of them said a word until the pot was empty and the bowls and spoons licked clean. Then the alchemist sat back in his chair and took a deep breath.

'There is one ingredient of the great work,' he said, 'that cannot be found in my laboratory.'

'Oh?' said Jack.

'Nor in any laboratory, for that matter. Yet without it no philosopher has any chance of success. It is called the *prima materia.*'

It was the straw that broke the camel's back. Jack's mind buckled beneath the weight of new information. Words tumbled around inside his head; alembic, magnesia, athanor, mercury. He couldn't remember what any of them meant. There was only one way to escape them, and Jack took it. Before the alchemist had even begun to explain, he was fast asleep on the chair where he sat.

Chapter Nine

JACK woke in darkness. The world was full of roaring and his mind was reeling with terrifying images of snakes and strange beasts, watched over by a man with wings on his heels. For a few, dizzy moments, he was utterly lost, with no idea at all of where he was. Then his gaze fell upon the dull glow of the dying embers and he remembered. The roaring sound was the alchemist snoring in the loft somewhere above his head.

Jack must have been snoring as well. His throat was sore and his mouth was wooden with thirst. He sucked on his tongue and tried to go back to sleep, but despite the warm blanket that the alchemist had wrapped around him as he slept, it was no use. Sooner or later he would have to get a drink.

The moon was quite bright, but the window was small and very little light came in to see by. Jack stood up and, treading warily, began to make his way across the room towards the scullery. The door was stiff, wedged on to the uneven stones of the floor. Jack had to put his shoulder to it, and it squawked horribly as it opened, causing Barnstable up in the loft to gasp in his sleep and turn over. When he was snoring comfortably again, Jack crept forward in the dark, reaching out with blind hands for the water crock. He found it with his toes. The water was cool and sweet and he drank deeply.

But by then, sleep had abandoned him. Instead of going straight back to his blanket, Jack crossed to the window of the scullery, drawn by the pale, clear light. The sky was frothy with clouds, but the face of the moon looked down between them and brought the surface of the river alive with gentle glints. On the other side, the grey land stretched away beyond seeing, so completely different from the daytime landscape that it filled Jack with a nameless dread. Out there, in every field, in every road and stream and hedgerow, Hermes and his mischief were waiting. It had been Hermes who sent him to sleep and caused the carts to get jammed, Hermes who had led him to the water's edge to find the philosopher's egg, Hermes who had brought him here to study his own, clandestine art.

Jack felt powerless in the face of such mystery, which seemed to roll away like the darkness towards infinity. His mind could cast no more illumination on it than a candle could cast on to the night landscape outside. The only comfort lay in the certainty that the alchemist understood. He would shelter Jack and teach him, until he could find his own way through the dark.

It was fully light when Jack woke. Barnstable was on his knees in front of the hearth, blowing gently on a couple of weakly glowing cinders and causing ashes to billow up in a fine cloud around his head. The night terrors had vanished and Jack felt surprisingly confident.

'If that's not puffing,' he said, 'I don't know what is.'

Barnstable laughed delightedly and knelt up. Jack slipped down on to the hearth beside him and together they snapped tiny beech twigs and fed them to the recalcitrant embers, which finally consented to burn.

'Damp sort of day,' said the alchemist. 'Gets into my old bones.' Still on his knees, he shuffled over to the nesting box and lifted the lid. 'Like to feed her?'

Jack nodded. The hen popped out and ruffled her feathers energetically, then ejected a sloppy white mess on to the floor behind her. Barnstable stood up and untied a small sack from a rope which hung from the beams above his head. Jack reached into it and took out a handful of oats. Kneeling down again in front of the hearth, he called to the hen. She regarded him coldly with one eye and shook herself again. He dribbled a few oats out on to the floor. She came over and pecked at them, then gobbled the rest from his open hand. The blunt stabbing of her beak made him giggle and squirm.

The alchemist looked on with a benign smile. The hen left

Jack and helped herself to water from a little dish beside the box. Then she ruffled herself once more, scolded the crackling twigs briefly and hopped back on to her nest.

Jack closed her lid. 'Can I feed the others outside?'

'With pleasure,' said Barnstable, handing over the oat sack. 'I'm beginning to wonder why I didn't take on an apprentice before.'

The day was overcast and drizzly, but Jack's good humour brightened it. He tried to feed the outside hens from his hands as well, but the cock flew at him and gave him a fright and he decided it would be safer to scatter the oats instead. Afterwards he wandered round the garden, rescuing some bean poles which had blown down in the night and collecting green windfalls from beneath the trees. The alchemist was so pleased that Jack found more work to do, filling the water crock with buckets from the well on the other side of the track and then bringing in enough firewood for two days. It was the kind of work he enjoyed, and by the time breakfast was ready he had almost forgotten the tedium of the laboratory and the confusion of all those new words. But Barnstable reminded him.

'Do you remember much of what I told you yesterday?'

'A little,' said Jack.

'Good. But it's of no consequence, really. Most of the things we discussed will be of no use to you until much later on in your apprenticeship.'

Jack looked up from his porridge and grinned with delight, but the alchemist's eyes seemed to lack their customary spark.

'It has been a pleasure having you around,' he said. 'You're a helpful lad and I could use someone to lighten the load on these old bones.'

Jack felt the cold shadow of Hermes creeping across the room. 'But I thought I was staying,' he said. 'I thought I was your apprentice.'

'You are, you are. And no matter what happens to you in life, you will always be my apprentice, even if you forget it yourself from time to time.'

Jack's mental fabric was beginning to fray around the edges again. 'Well, then . . .'

'You were very sleepy last night, weren't you?'

'Yes.'

'And perhaps you didn't hear what I told you about the *prima materia*?'

Jack looked glumly into his porridge. 'I might have been asleep. I don't remember.'

There was a long silence. Barnstable continued to eat his breakfast and Jack followed suit. Not until they had both finished did the alchemist speak again.

'The *prima materia*,' he said, 'is the basis of our art. It is the elemental matter from which the work begins. Without it, all our metals and powders and salts are quite worthless. Without it there is no alchemy. It is sometimes known as the stone of the philosophers, though it is not the same as the philosopher's stone, which can be fashioned from it. Within the *prima materia* spirit and matter come together and enter into conflict. He who holds it holds chaos. But only he who knows its nature can transmute it into gold.'

Jack didn't like the sound of it at all. He glanced round edgily. 'Where is it?' he asked.

Barnstable shrugged. 'Only you can know where your particular stone can be found.'

'You mean I have to go out and look for it?'

'That's right, yes.'

'But where? Where do I look for it?'

Again the alchemist shrugged. 'I don't know. But perhaps I can give you some clues. The stone, they say, lies alone in deep hollows, or in places where water has stopped running or else risen in flood. It can be found among the ashes of lost dreams or at the graveside of vanity. Dark places, Jack; *in stercore invenitur*. It is found in filth.'

There was a long silence. The fire had done its work and was dying down again. The drizzle trickled soundlessly down the window pane like tears. Jack stared at it until he could stand it no more.

'I don't even know what it looks like, this stone.'

'Nor do I,' said Barnstable. 'But you will, when you find it.'

There were more questions, but Jack knew that they wouldn't be answered, except by more of Hermes' trickery. He allowed the silence to descend again. In the hearth, the pile of embers shifted and collapsed into its own hollow heart. There was nothing left to wait for.

Chapter Ten

Jack caught a glimpse of the two birds through the dense crowd. They glared at each other from the restraints of their owners' arms. There were still people gathering round to inspect them both before making their bets. It was a good crowd for Jack's purpose. There was plenty of money about.

A murmur ran through the gathering and Jack pushed closer in towards the centre. The cockers were baiting the birds; swinging them at each other in a way designed to enrage them both. Jack felt the pressure of bodies around him as people pressed forward for a view of the action. He braced his elbows to give himself breathing-room, but other than that he kept still and quiet. He didn't mind the crush. It created ideal conditions for his work.

A man beside him jangled a pocketful of coins. 'Care for a penny on the speckled, Jim?'

Jack didn't hear the reply. There was a flurry in the ring as the cocks were released and everyone's attention turned towards them. The man shook the coins again. Jack didn't look up at him, but he allowed the shoving of the crowd to push him closer, so that his hip was pressed up tight against the man's leg. The speckled cock leapt forward, leaning back on his flapping wings, striking out with the iron spur tied to his leg. The red cock sprang up and clear, then landed a fine blow with his beak on top of his rival's head. Jack's fingers touched the stitched rim of the man's trouser pocket. The cloth was of good wool, close woven and warm. The cocks rose together, each of them striking, neither hitting home. They landed and rose again in a swirl of red and grey and iridescent green. Feathers were fluttering up into the air, and the crowd was roaring and pushing to get closer. Jack's hand slid home. His fingers made contact with the edges of the coins. A bit further and he would have them.

There was a hiss as the speckled cock got the advantage and forced the red one to the ground, going for its eyes. The cockers stepped in to separate them, and for some reason the man chose that moment to give his money another shake. But instead of the coins in his pocket, he discovered Jack's hand.

He turned, his mouth open in astonishment. Jack tried to pull away but his hand was trapped. He tugged harder. The cloth ripped and his hand came free, but it wasn't much help to him. He was hemmed in by spectators, and there was nowhere for him to go.

'You little swine!'

The flat of the man's hand caught Jack full in the side of the face. 'Pick my pocket, would you?'

The cockfight was forgotten, and the crowd parted with mysterious ease to create a new ring around Jack and his assailant who slapped him around the head a second time, then closed his hand into a fist and hit him full in the mouth. Jack fell on to the cobbles and tried to scamper away on all fours, but the man caught him by the collar and dragged him to his feet again. Jack heard the cloth rip and felt a cold draught across his back.

Two younger men waded in and tried to end the fight.

'Come off him, Barney. He's only a lad.'

But Barney wasn't in the mood to be restrained. If anything, his fury was increasing, and Jack was beginning to fear for his life.

Once more Barney hit him and knocked him down. Jack wrapped his arms around his head and waited for more, but it didn't come. A strange hush descended on the crowd and into it came the sound of a woman's voice.

'Shame on you, Barney,' it said. 'I would have thought you had more decency than to pick on a boy that size.'

Jack looked up. A tall, thin woman was standing with her back to him, facing Barney who was breathing hard but looking somewhat chastened.

'He was robbing me, Nell!' he said, but without the conviction that had caused his previous fury. Jack scrambled to his feet and tried to make a getaway, but Nell reached out and took him by the arm. Her fingers felt like the pincers Tom used to remove worn shoes from horses' hooves.

'Let me have a look at you.'

Jack gazed at her as she began to examine his face. Her accent was unlike any that he had heard in the surrounding districts. If it reminded him of anyone it was Master Gregory, and yet she wore clothes as plain as any of the townspeople around her. She seemed to have a natural authority as though she expected to be listened to and respected.

'Well,' she said, when she had finished her inspection of Jack's injuries. 'You've made a right mess of the lad. You've split his lip and knocked out his teeth and you may very well have broken his jaw as well. Fine work for a man of your size. Are you pleased with yourself?'

Barney looked thoroughly shamefaced, and it was clear that he didn't have much support among the crowd. Jack ran his tongue around his teeth. One of them was broken and hanging by a thread from his gum, but as far as he could tell it was the only one.

'Are you going to take him off and patch him up?' Nell continued.

Barney muttered and looked down at his feet.

'Well, cough up, then,' said Nell, 'so that somebody else can. You can't send the lad off like this, whatever he's done.'

There was no move from Barney, but Nell was not about to give in. 'Cough up a bit of that change, Barney. Before people start asking where it came from.'

With a disgusted grimace, Barney delved into his pocket and shoved a couple of coins into Nell's hand. Then he turned and stormed away through the crowd. Nell smiled and winked at Jack.

'You're a rogue,' she said, 'but not as bad a one as he is.'

Chapter Eleven

NELL led Jack through the damp backstreets of Shipley, stopping twice along the way to spend some of Barney's money on dried peas and a ham bone. Her house was in a row of small cottages, very similar to the one in which Jack had spent his childhood. Inside it was almost pitch dark until Nell opened the shutters and let in the gloomy daylight.

'Now, let's have a look at you,' she said, drawing him forward into the best of the light. Jack winced as she poked and prodded around the bruised tissues of his face, but her verdict was favourable.

'You'll live. That tooth will drop away in its own time. No sense in forcing it. Then you'll have to get a gold one, won't you?'

She laughed, but Jack wondered if he might, one day, when he had learnt how to make it. It would certainly look rather elegant.

'You still have a lot more than I have,' Nell went on, opening her mouth and revealing more gaps than teeth. 'But I don't mind it. There are many who would have given more than gold to live long enough to lose their teeth.'

Jack nodded, reminded of his dead brothers and sisters. Nell set about lighting the fire. 'You don't seem like a bad sort,' she said. 'I wouldn't say you were brought up to be a thief any more than I was.'

'No, I wasn't,' said Jack, remembering his mother's fierce sense of honour. For the first time he found himself wondering whether she had been right. Perhaps things might have been different. Perhaps one or two of the little ones might have been saved.

'I wasn't,' he said again, reeling away from the pain his thoughts were beginning to ignite.

'Then how did you come to it?' asked Nell.

Jack gazed at her blankly. He had, he realised, no conception whatsoever of how long it was since he had left the alchemist's warm fireside. It could have been weeks, months, even years. To begin with he'd had to survive on hedge berries and sour crab-apples and green hazelnuts, so that if his belly wasn't empty it was griping. He slept in the crooked arms of old oak trees or beneath thick, voley hedges, or under the skirts of hay-ricks which weren't too close to their owners' houses. There was some other kind of quest as well, which he found he had almost forgotten about. A search that made no sense to him now.

He had walked the roads and tracks, stopping to search for the mystical stone in foxy hollows and pig-ploughed paddocks, in brambly ruins and in sludgy ponds. Occasionally he would find an interesting possibility and drop it into the cherry bag. In quiet moments he would take it out and examine it, trying to convince himself that he had found what he was looking for. But it never worked. No matter how much he wanted to believe it, Jack could not manage to invest the stone with the magical properties he knew the *prima materia* must have.

So he carried on; he puddled and probed in hollows and fissures and trenches. He put his hands into rabbit holes, was chased out of badger setts, and was observed with perplexity by creatures both wild and domestic. He dug beneath trees and forgotten foundations, lifted flat stones and rolled back boulders. He investigated ring forts and hollow barrows, burrowed into muck heaps and wallowed in drains. He found worms and horse leeches, toads and newts; he found bits of rusted metal and shards of old pots. He found beautiful things; white and pink crystals, and a fish that some wizard had turned into stone. He hid them again in case he came back, and moved on, still searching, still hopeful.

But although the bag sometimes got quite full of strange and beautiful stones, it was always emptied again, sooner or later when it became too heavy, and Jack seemed never to come any closer to his goal. But he didn't stop believing. He was certain that sooner or later it would all be behind him; the searching and striving, the hunger pangs that he endured hour by hour, and day by day. He would find the *prima materia* and he would turn it into gold.

Nell was still watching him; waiting for an answer.

'I was hungry,' he said.

He had tried to earn his keep, but although he did his best to appear bright and cheerful when he went to someone's door to ask for work, it was clear from people's expressions that he was beginning to look as desperate as he felt. Time after time, his mind produced images of the beggar boys he had seen in the streets of London. He remembered their eyes, mean and hopeless, utterly lacking in pride. Whatever else happened, he couldn't bear to end up like that. Instead, he began to steal.

It was innocent enough at first; a few sweet apples from a twilight orchard or a bunch of carrots and a few potatoes from a cottage garden. Jack could easily convince himself that no one would even notice that they were gone. But then one day, he came upon a more tempting opportunity for theft.

It was late morning and he was passing down a quiet road between copses of oak and beech when he noticed a jacket hanging on a branch, just a few yards in off the road. He stopped and listened. Above the bubbly drone of the wood pigeons, he could just make out the sound of a saw, deep in the woods. He looked round, his heart in his mouth. Apart from the flies which darted erratically in and out of the sunlight, there was no movement at all. Slowly, carefully, Jack crept into the shadows, stopping every few paces to listen again. The saw stopped for a while, then started up again. A hornet lumbered by, inspecting several trees as though it were lost. Jack slunk forward and reached for the jacket.

He didn't know what he expected to find or what he intended to do, but when his exploring hand fell upon the pocket of the jacket he was left with no doubt. Inside it was a heavy slab of griddle bread wrapped in a piece of an old shirt. Before he knew what he was doing, Jack was back on the road again and heading for one of those hidden, gloomy places that by now he knew so well. The bread was hard and sour, but Jack was so famished that it tasted delicious. Afterwards he slept soundly for a couple of hours, and when he woke, he felt no remorse for what he had done. But hunger was a hard master and guilt was no match for it. Jack became bolder and more adroit, creeping into houses while the occupants were out working or even, occasionally, while they were sleeping. He hung around the market-places of the small towns he passed through, palming muffins or quinces or dried figs despite the vigilance of the stall-holders. He learnt to brush up against people by accident and slip a hand into their bag during the confusion. There was rarely anything in them that he could use, but on one occasion he came away with a smart tinder box, which he swapped in the next town for a whole jugged hare.

'Have you no family of your own?' Nell asked.

Jack told of his mother's death, and of being taken on as an apprentice by Tom. His words were a bit mumbly because of his broken tooth and swollen mouth, but he managed to tell the story of the cart accident and his flight to the river. Then he stopped, remembering in the nick of time that he was sworn to secrecy. Nell noticed his hesitation.

'And?' she said.

'And so I set out on my own.'

'You walked all the way to Yorkshire? Whatever for? There's a lot more pickings to be had in London, I would have thought.'

Jack shrugged. Nell emptied the peas into a dish and began picking through them for maggots and mouse droppings. For a long time neither of them spoke. The fire took heart and Jack moved closer to it. Nell finished with the peas and poured them into the pot around the ham bone.

'Would you like to hear my story?' she said.

Jack nodded politely. Nell settled the pot above the flames and pulled up a stool beside the hearth.

'I was born into great wealth,' she began. 'My great grandfather was a knight of the realm and was given half of Yorkshire by the king. Much of it had been sold off by my father's time, but he still owned thousands of acres of good land and a few grand houses besides. I grew up surrounded by servants; waited on hand and foot. I never wanted for anything. My life was mapped out for me before I was even born, and it would have been a comfortable one, you can be assured.'

She gazed into the fire and smiled at private memories, then sighed. 'But I was headstrong. I wouldn't have anyone else making my decisions for me. I ran off with a young tailor who often came to the house to make clothes for my brother, and I became his wife.' She smiled again, a little more wryly this time. 'He set up shop here in Shipley but for obvious reasons he couldn't do business for my father any more, nor for any of the local gentry, and it was a hard struggle. We survived though we lived in constant fear of discovery.'

'That's why you talk differently,' said Jack.

Nell laughed. 'Can you still hear it?'

'Yes. It's very clear to me. Everybody must know who you are.'

'A lot do, it's true. But no one ever gave me away and I'm grateful for that. Not that it matters any more. I'm dead and forgotten as far as my brother is concerned. It's all his, now.'

'What about your children? Do they know?'

'I only had one child,' said Nell. 'She died of consumption a few weeks after her father did.'

The information induced no sympathy in Jack. To acknowledge tragedy in the lives of others would have been to acknowledge his own, and that he could not do. Death was common; everyone had experience of it. Why give it power?

Nell, in any case, seemed to expect no response. 'I was too proud to go back to my family,' she continued, 'even though I was close to desperation. I struggled on my own for a while, but not for long. Another man came along and I married again. And when he died, I married again and here I am, wearing out a third husband!'

Jack looked around and noticed for the first time the evidence that a man lived there; a large pair of trousers hanging beside the chimney, a flat cap on the nail inside the front door.

It made him nervous. This latest husband might not take as kindly to young thieves as his wife did.

'You needn't worry,' said Nell. 'He won't be home for a day or two. He's a weaver and he's gone to buy fleeces in the market at Bradford. I'll give you a bed for the night while you forget about Barney, but you'll have to go in the morning.' She lifted the lid of the pot, which was just beginning to steam, and gave the contents a stir. 'Not that I wouldn't mind keeping you if it was up to me, since I have none of my own.'

Jack reflected that he wouldn't have minded being kept, at least for a while, but Nell's thoughts had moved on. For a moment she looked at the ground with a melancholy expression, then her face cleared and she smiled.

'I have no regrets,' she said. 'None at all. I've made my own decisions and I've stood by them, even when times were hard. I believe that we make our own happiness, Jack. In here.' She pointed to her breast as she spoke. 'We may not be able to control everything that happens outside us, but in here we are our own masters.'

She said no more but busied herself with dusting the pewter which stood on a narrow little dresser beside the door. Jack watched her, thinking about what she had said, but the warmth of the fire was soporific and before long his chin dropped on to his chest and he dozed off.

When Nell shook him awake, the daylight had gone and a pair of tallow candles burned on the mantel above the hearth. The first thing he was aware of was considerable pain around his cut and bruised face, but the smell of the pottage soon overcame it and he sat up eagerly.

'I made it good and soft for you,' said Nell, handing him a bowl. 'If you can't eat it you can drink it.'

Even that was not so simple, but the pain wore off as the meal went on, and things were made a lot easier when the loose tooth broke free of its moorings in his gum. He spat it out and threw it into the fire.

Nell said nothing until her bowl was empty. Then she sat back and sighed contentedly.

'That's why I don't want riches,' she said. 'When you have

everything it all tastes the same. There's nothing left to enjoy. But a bowl of good stew when you're hungry, now that's pleasure.'

Jack did not reply, and after a moment or two, Nell laughed. 'I don't suppose you'd agree with me, though, would you?'

Jack shrugged. The truth was that he was too intent upon the food to have an opinion either way. But Nell pressed on.

'You'd like to be rich, wouldn't you?'

Jack couldn't answer. The truth was that he had never considered it. There was a vague dream somewhere deep in the recesses of his unconscious mind, based upon fairy stories his mother had told them all when he was small. Happy ever after. It was nothing to do with real life.

'What if I could tell you how?'

'How what?'

'How to be rich?'

Jack experienced a silent groan in his heart like a nausea of the spirit. Why was it that the world wouldn't seem to leave him alone? Why did it have to keep pumping him up and then letting him down again? All the same, he sat up a little straighter and looked towards Nell with interest. She smiled and refilled his bowl.

'Not far from here,' she said, 'to the east of the town, where the best land is, there's a great house where a very wealthy man lives. He's a Duke, actually. His name is Neville Gordon. I'm not part of that world any more and I have no dealings with it, but I still have spies; I know what goes on. And this is what I have heard.'

There was a sudden scrape and flutter of bats in the eaves and Jack jumped, but Nell went on regardless.

'Gordon is a great breeder of horses. He is famous for his race horses throughout the length and breadth of England. People come from all over the country to bring mares to his stallions or to buy young stock. He is breeding up a strain he calls 'thoroughbred', which comes from crossing good English hunter mares with fleet, fine boned stallions from the East, across the seas. He has many sons and daughters of a horse called the Byerly Turk which was brought into the country about thirty years ago.'

Jack was frowning with the effort of trying to understand. He loved horses so much that he was willing to put up with a lot, but the string of unfamiliar words was having its usual effect on his mind. Nell seemed to appreciate his difficulties.

'But you needn't concern yourself with all that,' she said. 'All you need to know is that a few months ago Gordon went to Arabia himself and brought back a young stallion to breed with his mares. It was the talk of the whole county when it happened. But what isn't so well known, and is being kept very quiet, is that the horse has gone missing.'

'Gone missing?'

Nell nodded. The candles flickered and threw dim light into the poky corners. In the street outside, men's voices approached and receded again. Nell's eyes were bright, enjoying the effect her story was having on her guest.

'Gone missing,' she said. 'The colt was quite mannerly for some time after he arrived. The crossing would have tired him, no doubt, and the Duke took great pains to make sure he recovered his strength. It's possible that he pampered him too much, because he kicked a stable boy and broke his leg, then took off across the country and up on to the moors, jumping everything in his path. The party that set out to bring him back only succeeded in driving him further off, and for a long time there was no word of him at all.'

Jack's eyes were wide with curiosity. He remembered the fine, shining horses at Master Gregory's house, and although he wasn't sure what a moor was, his mind was conjuring up spectacular images of what it might be. Nell was clearly enjoying some private thoughts of her own, because she smiled to herself for a while before she continued.

'You can imagine the Duke's state of mind. He has lost the most wonderful horse he ever owned; a horse that he crossed the ocean to buy and bring home. But he can't tell anyone, you see?'

'Why not?'

'Because if it was widely known that such a valuable horse

was roaming free, all the thieves and rogues in the countryside would be out hunting for it, wouldn't they? And who knows where it might end up? No. He has kept very quiet about all this, Jack.'

'Then how do you know?'

'As I told you, I have my spies. And one of them has told me something very interesting indeed. The Duke, it seems, has made a quiet offer to a few trusted parties in the area. Anyone who catches the Arabian horse and brings it back safely will have the hand of his youngest daughter in marriage and a fine house with its own estate to go with her.'

Jack waited for more, but Nell was looking at him with shining eyes as though she, too, was waiting. 'Well?' she said at last.

'Well, what?'

'Aren't you interested?'

'I didn't know you could swap horses for people.'

Nell clucked impatiently. 'Oh, anything can be bought or sold at the right price,' she said. 'But you haven't understood, have you?'

'Understood what?'

'You could claim the reward, Jack. A fine young bride and a house and lands. You'd be rich, don't you see?'

Jack could see four candle flames reflected in Nell's eyes. He watched them for a while and realised that he was waiting for a sentence that began with 'but'. When it appeared that Nell had no more to say, he supplied it himself.

'But they wouldn't give them to me.'

'Why not? Trusted friend to trusted friend, that's how the message is passed on. A trusted friend gave it to me and I'm giving it to you. Neville won't go back on his word. He couldn't, without losing face. Among trusted friends, that is.'

Jack tried again. 'But I can't catch a wild Arabian horse. I couldn't even put the tack on old Dobbs properly. Even if I could get near him, he'd probably kill me.'

Nell shrugged indifferently. 'Then you'd better not try,' she said. 'Tell someone else who has more courage and let them try. If you don't believe in yourself there's no sense in undertaking anything, is there? But I'll tell you this. Sooner or later someone will do it and it could just be someone like you. Someone with nothing to lose and everything to gain. Someone who can use their wits and think of a different way of doing things.'

Jack wasn't sure whether to feel offended or ashamed. 'Why are you telling me all this?' he asked.

'Because I thought you might still be young enough to believe in a dream,' said Nell. 'But perhaps I was wrong. Perhaps you're not.'

Chapter Twelve

THAT night, Jack found it difficult to sleep. His bed was up in the loft, beneath the eaves where bats came and went throughout the night. He could hear the flubber of their leathery wings sometimes so close that he could feel the breeze on his cheeks, but it was not that which kept him awake. Nor was it his jaw which, although stiff, was no longer very painful. He had spent too long dozing in front of the fire and now his mind was fully alert.

Nell was sleeping on the settle in the chimney corner in the room below. As Jack listened to her regular breathing, he couldn't stop thinking about the horse roaming loose on the moors. His imagination created a hundred possibilities for him, some ending in triumph and others in failure. But after each one the same doubts returned. Why should he believe such an unlikely story? He knew nothing about Nell, after all. Perhaps her head was full of all kinds of wild imaginings? It would be absurd to go tearing off into the wilderness with nothing more to go on than her word.

When he did eventually fall asleep, he dreamt that he was outside the alchemist's house, looking for eggs in the bushes and the hidden corners of the sheds where the hens chose to nest. He searched long and hard without success until at last he found a single smooth, white egg. He was jubilant, and ran into the house with his prize. But it wasn't the alchemist's house any longer. It was his mother's house and Matty was curled up in the chimney corner, gazing out with sunken eyes.

Jack approached him, holding out the white egg. But Matty was too sick. He turned his face to the wall. The egg dropped from Jack's fingers and fell towards the ground.

Before it could land and break, Jack woke. He was alone in the dark little roof space above Nell's parlour, and he was sweating, gasping for breath. He pulled his blanket round his head and entreated sleep to return but it would not.

In the morning he slipped quietly down from the loft, taking care not to waken Nell, who was still snoring softly on the settle. The blanket that the alchemist had given him was draped over a wooden clothes-horse beside the fire. For the first time in weeks it was dry.

Jack went out into the yard and stood in the damp morning, looking up at the dark range of hills which loomed above the little town. They were gloomy and forbidding, but at the same time infused with a sense of mystery which sent a tingle through his bones. It was Hermes, he knew, trying to lure him on again, and for a long moment he wished that he had gone back to Tom and taken what was coming to him.

What did it mean, to follow a dream? Jack's dreams were all like the one he'd had a few hours before; night terrors which shocked him awake and left him staring into the darkness. Could there be another kind of dream? A good kind? Perhaps there were other ways of making gold?

Inside the house, Nell woke and coughed. Jack gave her time to get up and dressed, then went back inside. She was yawning, still sitting on the edge of the settle, still in her night clothes.

'Morning, Jack.'

'Morning.'

'You'll be off, then.' It wasn't a question.

'I suppose I will, yes.'

'Good lad. I'll give you what's left of Barney's cash. You can do what you like with it.' Her face was tired and lifeless, still puffy with sleep. She lifted her skirt from the stool where it lay and untied a kerchief stitched on to the waistband. 'There you are. Do what you like with it.'

Jack took the small coins she offered.

'Not enough?' said Nell, with slight irritation.

'It's plenty,' said Jack.

'Off you go, then. There's no use you hanging around here, is there?'

'I suppose not.' Jack picked up his blanket and moved

across the room. Beyond the open door, blocking the sky completely, the dark moors stretched away. Could there really be a horse up there? Did he dare to dream it?

He turned and looked back at Nell.

'Where shall I find the horse?' he asked.

Nell smiled and sparks of delight freshened her eyes. 'That's my boy, Jack,' she said.

Chapter Thirteen

JACK spent most of his money before he left the town. He bought two pound loaves from the baker and a piece of butter and a good wedge of cheese from a farm girl at the corner of the street. Then, following Nell's directions, he set out up the steep, cobbled streets towards the moors.

The rain cleared and was replaced by a sharp, cold wind, which dried the ground beneath Jack's feet but cut through his clothes and made him shiver. Before long he had left the town behind him and was walking up narrow cart roads between high walls of grey stone. Behind them, steep, muddy fields ran up to small farmhouses and cottages which huddled in against the hillsides like sleeping animals. The wind blew the smoke sideways from their chimneys.

The higher Jack climbed, the harder and colder it seemed to blow. From time to time he rested in a stand of trees or in a sheltered corner where two walls met. He was determined to make his provisions last as long as possible, but the cold made him ravenous and he could rarely resist nibbling at the fresh crust of his bread. By the time he reached the top of the hill which overlooked Shipley, half of the first loaf was gone.

It was mid-afternoon and the wind was still blowing hard, finding the gaps between the stones in the walls and moaning through them. The road levelled off and ran straight along the edge of the moors. Jack followed it as far as he could, reluctant to cross the last boundary wall which separated the hillside farmland from the bleak, rushy expanse of the heath. It seemed impossible that any creature, man or beast, would choose to inhabit a landscape like that, even if it meant freedom. It occurred to him that the horse might be dead, and he considered abandoning the whole venture and returning to the relative comfort of the town streets below. But when the road began to slope away again, back down towards the brighter green of better land, he had to come to a decision. The dream of Matty replayed itself in his mind, causing his heart to lurch and carrying him, almost involuntarily, towards the wall. As he climbed it he knew that there was, in fact, no choice, and never had been. Hermes was watching over everything, singing with the thin voice of the wind, drawing him on towards the unknown.

For the rest of that day, Jack wandered aimlessly across the cold, squelching boglands, his direction guided only by the need to keep the relentless wind at his back. The landscape was huge and empty, each horizon yielding to another equally desolate, equally lacking in promise. Ragged crows tumbled in the wind like huge smuts. Thin sheep hugged the cover of slopes and left indignantly when Jack disturbed them. Other than that, nothing moved except Jack himself, small and lonely beneath the indifferent sky.

As night began to fall, he found scant shelter among some stunted willow trees beside a sludgy black stream. There was brief comfort in the meal he made of bread and butter and cheese, but it didn't last for long. His blanket was poor protection against the cold and throughout the night, curled up like a stray dog, Jack shivered and shook and gritted his teeth to stop them from chattering. The chill fingers of exposure groped for him, but he fought them off, hugging himself, determined to survive.

Some time before dawn, the wind dropped and clouds settled on to the hills like thistledown. At first light, Jack got up. The chances of finding a horse in those conditions were negligible, and yet Jack had only two alternatives. He could stand still and get colder and wetter than he already was, or he could move on. So throughout the morning he walked within a dome of mist, with no idea of where he was going. Several times he came dangerously close to dark, murky bog holes, and once he blundered into the edge of a marsh which sucked with frightening power at his feet. After that he followed the faint tracks laid down by moorland creatures that were, in this hostile environment, much wiser than he. He never saw them, though. He saw no sign of life at all apart from the occasional sheep, shambling off into the white haze as though it were part of it.

During the afternoon the mist lifted and a weak, wintry sunlight replaced it. It did not, however, reveal any sign of the missing horse. Jack scanned the horizon constantly, veering towards vague shapes that might have been horses sleeping or grazing, but always turned out to be rocks or trees. His supplies were beginning to run short, and the lack of sleep began to cause giddy episodes, when the dreary surroundings twisted and tumbled and produced strange images in front of his eyes.

As the evening light began to fade, a hint of frost entered the still air, causing Jack to double his blanket and wrap it round his shoulders like a shawl. He was beginning to despair of finding shelter, when he found the land beginning to slope downwards again and revert to rough pasture and stone walls. He entered a small valley, at the head of which, nestling in the cleft between two steep hills, was a single, sturdy farmhouse. Wood-smoke hung on the air around it and Jack could smell it from where he stood. Fire was a luxury he could not expect, but the farm buildings which surrounded the yard would be good enough for him.

Dogs would be the problem, but Jack had learnt a lot over the last weeks and months. He waited until the darkness was complete, then walked slowly down towards the farm. With a stealth born of desperation he slipped soundlessly over loose stone walls and across the holding pens until he was at the edge of the yard. A strip of soft lamplight showed through a gap in the shutters of the house, but there was no sound at all. Nor was there any movement in the yard. The dogs were either in the house or asleep.

Barely breathing, Jack climbed into the yard and slipped like a shadow over the bottom door of the cow byre. Inside, a placid milker lay on a bed of dried rushes. When she saw Jack she lifted her head and regarded him with curiosity for a moment before accepting him as she accepted all other human eccentricity. Jack lay down beside her. She resumed her chewing of the cud and, lulled by the rhythmic sound and the solid warmth of her flank, he was soon sound asleep.

Chapter Fourteen

JACK woke to the musical ringing of milking. He turned on to his back, torpid in the fuggy warmth of the byre, but he wasn't allowed to sleep again. A cold nose nuzzled and a warm tongue licked his cheek.

'That's it, Rufus. You wake him up.' It was a girl's voice, light and humorous. Jack sat up. They were all looking at him; the girl with her cheek to the cow's flank, the dog who was now sitting down with his head on one side and the cow herself, still placidly chewing. The froth in the bucket was rising towards the rim.

'Ah, now he's awake,' said the girl. 'But where has he sprung from, that's the question.' There was a sly smile in her face as she spoke that Jack found quite enchanting. He didn't feel threatened in the slightest.

'We don't get many strays around here,' the girl went on. 'You're a fair step from home, I dare say.'

Jack scratched his head and nodded. From the yard a man's voice called out, 'Who are you talking to, Jenny?'

All three faces turned away from Jack and towards the door. The girl put a finger to her lips. 'Just Parsley, Father. She's imagining flies again.'

Footsteps crossed the yard and a door closed. 'He's not so bad,' Jenny whispered. 'But he has a bit of a temper in the mornings.' For a while she said nothing, but drew the last drops from the cow's udder and put the bucket up on to the window ledge, out of reach of the hopeful Rufus. Jack watched her surreptitiously. Her uncombed hair hung in long, gleaming shanks, snarling here and there in the rough wool of her jersey. Her face glowed with a healthy blush and seemed set in a permanent smile.

'If you had any milk to spare, I could buy it,' said Jack, making a weak jingle with the last two coins in his pocket.

Jenny looked around, slyly. 'I'll give you some,' she said, 'but only if you tell me what you're doing here.'

Jack shrugged. 'Just sleeping.'

'Not here, stupid. Here.' She gestured towards the world beyond the byre. 'Out here. Nobody comes here without a reason.'

She waited for a moment or two, and when Jack said nothing, she reached for the handle of the bucket. 'No milk, then.'

'Wait.'

'Tell me, then.'

Jack stood up and moved closer. 'Can you keep a secret?'

The girl nodded. Half a dozen hens had gathered at the open door and were crooning to each other inquisitively. Jenny made a half-hearted kick at them and they wandered away again. Rufus was sniffing at the corner of Jack's blanket where the last of his bread and cheese were tied. He hitched it up out of reach and stroked the dog's head. Then, in a low voice, he said, 'I'm here looking for a horse.'

Jenny burst into peals of laughter, covering her mouth to try and keep them contained.

'Why is it funny?'

'It's no secret,' said Jenny, still giggling. 'Everybody knows about that stupid horse. The whole country is out marching up and down the place looking for him.'

'Well, I haven't seen them,' said Jack.

'Maybe not. But we've had more visitors here in the last two weeks than in the last two years.' She laughed again. 'And the best of it is that they all think they have a secret.'

Jack's heart sank. 'Did anyone find him yet?'

Jenny shook her head. 'I don't think so. And I'll tell you something else for nothing. He's not far from here.'

'How do you know?'

'Because our mare has disappeared, our work horse, Bessie. Father's furious. He thinks she has run off with the stallion, see, because he found two sets of tracks. And if she has, they can't be far away. She would always hang towards home . . .' she blushed and giggled, '. . . no matter how handsome her sweetheart might be.'

'Didn't your father follow the tracks?'

'Of course he did. We all did. But you know what the mist was like yesterday. The tracks disappeared and the horses with them. We searched all day.'

'Maybe someone else has found them,' said Jack, glumly.

'Maybe. Maybe not.' Jenny reached for the bucket again and handed it to him. Rufus pricked up his ears. The froth had been deceptive. Now that it had settled, Jack could see that the milk only filled a quarter of the bucket.

'Don't take too much or you'll get me into trouble. And don't spill it.'

With great care, Jack tilted the bucket and began to drink. He didn't intend to be greedy, but it was difficult to stop once he had started, and Jenny had to prise the milk away from him.

'You'd better go,' she said. 'I might even see you later on, up there.' She gestured vaguely towards the hills.

Jack looked at his feet. 'Thanks for the milk. And for not telling anyone.'

Jenny nodded. 'Even if you can't catch the colt,' she said, 'you might find our Bessie. She's an old softy, she wouldn't give you any trouble.' She reached for a coil of dusty rope that was hanging from a bent nail in the rafters, then blushed and grinned charmingly. 'You can use this to catch her. But don't be expecting any daughter's hand in marriage from my father, you hear?'

Now it was Jack's turn to blush. He took the rope, screwed up his blanket into a clumsy ball and made a rush for the door. A moment later, without any idea of where he was going, he was out of the yard and climbing the steep hill behind the house towards the open heath. He did not look back.

At the top of the hill he paused to get his breath and look around. The black moorland rolled and dipped away in three directions. There were a hundred places where a pair of horses could be concealed, but at least the air was clear and he could see right to the horizon. And as he set out on his third day of searching, he had a new confidence. He now knew for certain that the Arabian colt did exist and was not just a figment of Nell's imagination.

The wind picked up again as the morning wore on as cold as on the first day, if not colder. Jack allowed himself to be guided by the little sheep tracks that skirted the bogs and ran around the contours of hills, going in any direction that seemed likely or even possible. Sometimes he climbed to high ground to get a broader view of the surroundings and sometimes he kept to the dells whose turns and deviations provided perfect cover for fugitive creatures. From time to time he called the mare's name, softly: 'Bessie, Bessie.' A dozen times he found what he thought was the imprint of a horse's hoof in the rough turf, but he could never be certain and he never found more than one at a time. The day was hard and frustrating, but it was softened by the memory of Jenny's smile. He had never really noticed girls before, but now he began to wonder what it really meant to be married. He remembered the pictures of the courtship between the Red King and the White Queen in the alchemist's house and they reminded him of his other search, for the mystical stone. The desolate surroundings provided hundreds of possibilities, but the idea of slopping around in those cold, wet bogs gave Jack the shivers.

To his combined pleasure and disappointment, Jack saw no sign of other searchers: if Jenny's family had come out again, they must have taken a different direction. He finished the cheese and all but one last crust of his bread at midday, sitting on the highest ground that he could find and exposed to the worst of the wind. Nothing moved, nothing disturbed that vast, dismal scene, and Jack was reduced to solitude again.

The day wore on and passed the eerie afternoon hour which marked the turn towards evening. Jack was beginning to wonder where he would sleep that night when something made him stop in his tracks. For a moment or two he had no idea what it was; he had seen nothing and heard nothing and the moors were as bleak and empty as ever. Then it came again. The wind was carrying the smell of horses.

But from where? And how far? For a few minutes Jack stood and looked around him in confusion, but at last he began to think more clearly and made the simple decision to walk straight into the wind. It was colder than ever now and he noticed that it bore a few frosty flecks of snow which stung his eyes and cheeks. The smell did not come consistently and at times he thought he must have imagined it. But it always came again, carried on the softer little gusts, and then it didn't need to any more. On the other side of a nearby rise in the ground was a dark, rushy mire and on the nearest edge of it was the huge, round form of Jenny's work-horse, Bessie. She whickered nervously to Jack as he appeared in her vision, as though she were relieved to see someone coming, and she stood quite still as he walked up to her. She even dropped her head to let him slip the rope around her neck. But of the Arab colt, there was no sign.

'Did someone find him, Bessie?' said Jack. 'Did they take him away and leave you here on your own?'

The mare nudged him anxiously with her nose, nearly knocking him down, and making him drop his last, grimy crust. He picked it up and broke off a piece for her. She took it and mumbled it around in her mouth but dropped it again, all green and slobbered. Jack didn't mind. He was delighted to have found her. Fancy houses and Dukes' daughters were for other kinds of people. Bessie suited Jack just fine. Whatever else happened, he was sure to get a meal and a night out of the snow.

'Come on, lady. We'd better get you home before it's too dark. Do you know the way?' He turned and pulled on the rope but the mare didn't follow. Instead she let out a shrill whinny that rang out across the heath and almost deafened Jack. He was about to protest when he heard a reply, short and feeble, more of a grunt than a whinny.

He was there; Jack saw him, or what little of him there was to be seen. He was not more than a few yards away, but it was no surprise that Jack hadn't noticed him before. The whole of his hind end was submerged in the mire. Only his head and shoulders were above it. The grass and rushes around his forelegs had been scrabbled into a muddy slush, but the ground must have been firmer there for he was still clinging on.

Jack stared, stunned by having found the colt and by the danger he was in, but most of all by the sheer beauty of the animal. He was wet, muddy, and clearly exhausted, but even so the clean lines of that noble head, the small ears, the soft, inward arch of his nose filled Jack with awe. He had never seen anything like it before.

'Bessie,' he whispered, 'we have to get him out.' It was nothing to do with marriages or fine houses; nothing to do with reward of any kind. All Jack knew was that a creature as beautiful as that could not be allowed to perish.

But he couldn't do it alone. Even if he could get a rope around the colt's neck, he would have no chance of pulling him out. He had to get help. More urgently this time he tugged at Bessie, but still she refused to follow. With a speed and dexterity that would have amazed Tom, Jack knotted the rope into a halter around the mare's head and, grabbing a handful of her coarse mane, pulled and wriggled his way up on to her broad back, dropping his bread again, leaving it for the crows. In quiet desperation he kicked, then hammered with his heels at the taut drum of Bessie's ribcage. Nothing would induce her to move. She was not going to abandon her young sweetheart and Jack was powerless to change her mind. He threw himself off her back and landed running, heading back the way he had come. He had taken no bearings during the day, but instinct came to his aid and he found that he could remember the shapes of the hills and hollows and the character of paths he had trodden before. He ran without stopping until he was out of breath and then he ran without it. His lungs hurt, his legs were like lead but he was going to make it. He had to.

Chapter Fifteen

Mrs Keithly, Jenny's mother, was shutting the hen-house door in the last gloom of dusk when Jack came hurtling down the steep hillside, lost his footing and landed in a heap on the roof of the pig-sty. He was so exhausted that he couldn't move, and she had to call her husband to carry him into the house.

'What happened to you, lad?' he asked, but Jack hadn't the breath to reply. It was some minutes before he was able to speak and then, with the whole family gathered around him, he gasped out the story.

'And how did you know Bessie's name and who she belonged to?' said Mr Keithly.

Jack looked guiltily at Jenny, who turned towards the corner with a shy smile. Her father registered it, but decided it was not worth pursuing.

'Will the colt last until morning?' he asked.

'I don't know. I don't think so.'

'Then we'd best act. Can you find the way back?'

Jack remembered the colt's fine, delicate head and the quiet patience of his suffering. 'I think so,' he said. 'I'll have to. We have to get him out.'

The rescue party was blessed with a clear night and an early-rising moon which was just waning from the full. Mr Keithly walked in front, leading the weary Jack on a spritely little grey pony, sure-footed as a goat on the narrow paths. Behind them came two of Jenny's brothers with a second pony laden with creaking baskets which held the tackle that would be needed to pull the colt out. This time Jack was sure of the way, even in the dark, and was able to bypass some of his earlier meanderings and take a more direct line. Even so it seemed to take forever. The young Keithlys chattered to each other in excitement for the first mile or two, then fell into the same dogged silence as their father. The moon rose higher, and Jack could sense Hermes reposing in the shadows it cast behind hills and hummocks, watching with a crafty smile. There was no knowing what he planned for them that night.

Although the snow was still little more than a threat, they were all chilled to the bone by the time Bessie heard them coming and called out a welcome. The grey pony recognised her voice and replied with a piercing whinny. To Jack's delight there was a third call, short and frail, but proof that the colt was alive.

The farmer and his two sons stood beside their mare and looked out into the bog. Jack felt proud to be with them and wondered whether his own brothers might have been a little like these boys, had they lived. 'There he is, see?' he said, pointing. 'Isn't he beautiful?' The colt was no further enmired than when Jack had last seen him, but the farmer's face was grave as he assessed the situation.

'It's not going to be easy,' he said. 'Not easy at all.'

He thought for a moment more, then turned to the pack pony and took something out of one of the baskets. It was a roller, a broad band of heavy leather fitted with a variety of rings and buckles, designed for breaking young horses. He handed it to Jack.

'You're going to have to do this now, lad,' he said. 'You're the lightest of us, and in any case, it's your business, not ours.'

Jack slipped down from the pony and Keithly handed him the roller. 'I don't know if it'll be possible, but you'll have to try.' As he spoke he was busy with a coil of strong rope, working the loose end free. 'This is for you, not the horse.' He tied it tightly around Jack's chest, under the armpits. 'So we can get you out if you start to go under. You've no idea how hard these bogs can pull once they get hold of you.'

Jack shuddered, remembering the sucking on his feet. He might have had a narrow escape already.

'What you have to do,' the farmer was saying, 'is try and get that roller round the colt's middle. There's no other way to get him out. If we try and pull him out by his head we'll only break his neck. So you'll have to try and dig under him, like. Do you understand?'

Jack understood, but he wasn't sure that he could carry it out. The colt's withers were above the surface of the bog, but his chest was far beneath it. Somehow he would have to get the roller down under him and pull it through to the other side to buckle it. From where he was standing it looked impossible.

'Off you go, then. No use waiting around.'

Jack began to walk forward, but Keithly pulled on the rope to stop him.

'On your belly, lad! Otherwise you'll just go straight under. Lie down and slither across. Spread the weight.'

Reluctantly, Jack did as he was advised. Immediately the freezing damp of the marsh soaked into his clothes and chilled the marrow in his bones. But a moment later he had forgotten about it, so hard was he concentrating on the work ahead of him. His worst fear, he realised, was that when he got close the horse would panic and struggle, sinking himself further; entirely, perhaps. As though the farmer knew what he was thinking, he called out from the bank. 'Quietly, Jack. Talk to him. You must always talk to a horse.'

No one had ever told him that before, but Jack realised that he knew it to be true. The best horsemen he had seen in the streets of London had always been talking to their animals, coaxing and approving and encouraging. The moonlight caught the bright black eye of the colt, turned towards him as he crawled spreadeagled. He stopped. He had peat in his mouth. He didn't know what to say.

'Shall I put Bessie's collar on?' asked one of Keithly's sons.

'Not until she has something to pull,' his father replied.

Jack found his tongue. 'You're a great lad,' he said softly. 'You're the finest horse I've ever seen and I'm not going to let you die, you hear?' He edged forward as he spoke, elbows and knees squelching on the treacherous surface. 'Don't you be afraid, now. It's only Jack. I'm a runaway, too, like you. But this isn't freedom that you've found, is it?' He hardly knew what he was saying, but he was getting closer. The horse surveyed him impassively, as though he knew that neither of them had much choice in the matter. 'Don't be scared, now.

Whatever happens next it has to be better than this, doesn't it?'

Jack's limbs were sinking deeper. The last few yards were like swimming through icy porridge. It took tremendous effort, but no matter how hard he was panting, he still spoke to the horse. 'Nearly there, now . . . stay quiet . . . beautiful boy . . . nearly there.' His hand made contact with the colt's neck. He felt hard muscle beneath the matted coat. 'Have you out of here . . . in no time . . .'

'Well done, Jack,' called Keithly. 'Take your time now. Quietly does it.'

Jack planted the roller on the colt's withers where they emerged from the sludge. The colt shook his head and clawed at the mud with his forelegs until he realised that it was still as futile as it had been before. He calmed down again as Jack prattled on. 'Woah, lad. Easy, now. Settle down. We'll get you out, you see if we don't.' He took the buckle end of the strap and began to push it down into the peaty soup beside the horse's ribcage. It went down easily, but Jack's arms weren't long enough to reach down to the bottom of the colt's chest. He tried to dig a hole but the surrounding mire just flowed back into it again. His face was in the mud and he was gasping and spluttering and spitting black mouthfuls into the darkness. He stopped to get his breath.

There was no sound from the watchers beneath the lee of the hill; no sound to be heard at all, apart from the combined breathing of himself and the horse. But Jack heard it nonetheless, the mocking laughter of Hermes as he looked on and saw the absurdity of mortal endeavour. For a moment he thought it meant the end, signalling another failure. But Keithly's voice dispelled his impending despair.

'Take your time, Jack. You're not beaten yet.'

'I can't get it down far enough!' he called back.

'You will, you will. Don't rush it. And keep talking to him.'

Jack found the breath to gabble again, any sort of nonsense that came into his mind. Soon afterwards his energy returned and he resumed his battle with the bog. Each time he pushed on the roller he managed to get it a little deeper, but never quite deep enough. As his strength waned he began to hear Hermes again, chuckling with the voice of the wind, and with sudden determination not to be defeated, he upended himself like a duck in a pond. With his bare feet waving in the air, he thrust himself downwards until his fingers, still grasping the roller, reached the bottom of the horse's chest. He grabbed the rope to pull himself back up, and on the bank, Keithly lent a hand.

'Got there?' he called.

Jack nodded, sobbing for breath. 'Halfway,' he called.

Still talking to the colt, he slipped over his submerged back to the other side. 'We'll soon have you out, now. I'll eat my hat if we don't. Or I would if I had one.'

He took a deep breath and repeated his diving act. On the third attempt his fingers found the buckles and on the fourth he grasped them and hauled them up. A minute later the roller was tightly fastened round the colt's girth and a cheer went up from the Keithlys as they swung into action.

Bessie behaved quite differently now that her boss was there. She moved willingly wherever he asked her to and soon she was tacked up and ready to do what she did best; pull.

'Now, lad,' said Keithly. 'Can you untie that rope from around your middle?'

Jack's hands were numb with cold, but the knot relinquished itself easily enough.

'Good. Now tie it good and tight on to the roller up there on his withers.'

Jack did as he was told, his frozen fingers slow and fumbling. When he was finally satisfied with his work he called out. 'But how will I get out?'

'On his back,' said the farmer.

'On his back?'

'Behind the roller.'

'But . . .'

'But nothing. Catch hold of his mane and hold on tight. He'll be too tired to even notice you're there.'

Jack acquiesced. The colt's mane was a lot sparser than Bessie's, but he collected two good hanks of it and wrapped them round his hands. His knees sunk into the mire around the horse's flanks.

'Ready?'

'Ready.'

'Right. Here we go. Hup, Bessie.'

The mare stepped forward and took up the slack in the rope, then leant her massive bulk into the collar. The roller tightened and stretched beneath Jack's thighs and the wither pad lifted. He found himself praying to Hermes not to let it break; not to let them all down at this final hour. And it seemed that, for once, his prayers were answered. As he felt himself moving, the colt scrabbled with his forelegs, digging out chunks of peat and rushes with his feet and flinging them past Jack's knees into the mire.

'Steady, Bessie. Easy now.'

The colt's head went up and down as he struggled harder and Jack hung on to his mane for all he was worth. Then suddenly, with a great, tearing squelch, they were free. The colt staggered and stumbled on to his knees but somehow regained his balance, then leapt and plunged across the last few sucking yards until he reached firm ground. Bessie whickered and turned to welcome him, nose to nose.

Keithly untied the rope and recoiled it. 'Fine foal she'll have if she's taken from him,' he said.

The other two laughed, but Jack was dumbstruck. The farmer had been right. The colt was alive and well, but he was trembling with exhaustion and cold. Whatever was on his mind now did not include Jack, who sat astride him as though he were old Dobbs. Nor did he resist when Keithly stepped quietly up to him, slipped a halter over his head and handed the lead rope to Jack.

'Now,' he said. 'Let's get moving again.' He turned to the boys who were holding the two ponies out of the way. 'You two get home and take the ponies with you. Jack and I can keep going and get that fellow home before he gets troublesome again.'

With surprising agility he sprang up on to Bessie's back and set her off along the edge of the bog. And as though he were still tied to her, the colt followed.

Chapter Sixteen

It was fully light the next morning and snowing hard when the strange pair rode into the Duke's stable yard. No one made a move to stop them. Even though the Arabian colt was mud-covered, snow-flecked and wobbling with exhaustion, it was impossible to mistake him for any other horse. Stable boys scattered to get his loose box set fair and heat water for a mash. A runner was dispatched to the house to inform the Duke. Then the head groom took the halter rope from Jack's numb fingers.

'Well done, lad. Down you get, now.'

Jack was about to comply, but Keithly had other ideas. 'Stay where you are,' he said, his voice calm and authoritative. 'We have some business to settle with the Duke before any reins are handed over.' He moved Bessie's imposing bulk closer to Jack and the colt, and the groom backed off.

'The horse has had a bit of a scare and got cold,' he went on. 'He needs some attention, but he'll last another few minutes.'

There was a commotion at the back gates of the yard and the Duke appeared in his dressing gown, escorted by a pair of elderly deer-hounds and closely followed by most of the household staff. He had eyes for nothing but the Arab colt and he stood for a long time in silence, appraising his condition. Jack sat quite still, trying to be invisible, trying not to look and feel like a thief. Nothing moved in the stable block except for the dogs which snuffled around in the piles of freshly-swept snow. Eventually the Duke looked up, not at Jack, but at Keithly.

'I know you, don't I?' he said.

'Indeed, you do,' said the farmer. 'I'm Adam Keithly and my father was John. Your father settled lands upon mine for service rendered to him, if you remember. I met you on many occasions when we were boys.'

Gordon nodded thoughtfully. 'I think you had the better of me in the steeplechase once or twice,' he said.

Keithly laughed. 'I did, but not often. And we no longer keep good horses. The land is only fit for sheep and cattle.'

The Duke looked slightly embarrassed. 'In any event,' he said, 'I thank you for bringing back my horse. How might I repay you?'

'By giving me a good breakfast, sir,' said Keithly. 'And as for the lad here, you can settle the Musgrave estate upon him.'

Gordon's face fell and he turned to look at Jack. Gradually his jaw dropped and an expression of horror came into his eyes. With an effort of will he composed himself and turned back to Keithly.

'We'll find something for the lad, of course,' he said. 'Would he like a pony, perhaps? There's a grand little gelding that my youngest has just grown out of.'

Keithly shook his head, and the look in his eyes permitted no compromise. 'Your daughter's hand and the Musgrave estate,' he said. 'That was the prize, and the lad will accept it.'

Jack closed his eyes and wished he could disappear into the darkness behind them. The world seemed to be full of a great roaring, but when he dared to look again there was no sound at all. Instead there was a ghastly hush as the Duke stared straight at him with a look akin to hatred on his face.

The colt moved restlessly, as though he, too, was made uneasy by the atmosphere. Jack slipped down from his back and hid behind him, away from the Duke's scornful gaze.

Keithly broke the silence. 'It's all fair and square. The boy hunted long and hard for the horse and he was the one to find him. He has brought him back alive and well, as you specified in your offer. There would seem to be no doubts outstanding. We all know you wouldn't go back on your word.'

Jack peeped out beneath the colt's neck. Gordon was red in the face and seemed to be struggling with some terrible anguish. He wanted to relieve him of it, to refuse any reward at all, but to do so would have been to undermine his friend, the farmer, and that he could not do. The Duke took a deep breath and seemed to come to some sort of decision.

'Listen, Adam,' he said. 'Why don't you and I step inside and have a talk about this?'

But Keithly was unyielding. 'There's nothing to talk about,' he said. 'Does the boy get the reward or doesn't he?' When the Duke still said nothing, he added, 'I assume this is the horse you're looking for, is it, Neville?'

Gordon was defeated. 'Yes, yes. Of course it is.' He turned to the nearest stable boy and bellowed at him. 'What are you waiting for? Get the colt inside and rugged up before he dies of the cold!'

The yard erupted into action, with people everywhere racing for buckets and brushes and straw. Keithly turned to Jack and winked at him with a broad smile of satisfaction.

'I'll have that breakfast, if you don't mind,' he said to the Duke. 'The snow is settling fast and I'm a long way from home.'

Jack and the farmer were given a huge breakfast in the kitchens at the back of the great house. It was a wonderful meal after the long, freezing ride, but there was something about Keithly's demeanour that troubled Jack. He was far more satisfied than he ought to have been.

'One of your boys could have had this,' Jack said.

'The breakfast?'

Jack nodded. 'And the rest. I can't marry his daughter, we all know that.'

'Oh, but you can, Jack. And you will. Mind, now, if you get any trouble you tell me, hear?'

'But I couldn't have brought back the horse without you. The reward is as much yours as mine.'

'No, it isn't. And in any case, I want none of this big house muck, nor I don't want it for any of my lads. My father was sold short by this family, but what I have out of it is good enough for me and for my boys. We have all we need.' The satisfied smile returned to his face and he went on, 'And you will have all you need, and more. And as for the Duke, I imagine he'll be a while living this down.' He laughed out loud and stood up to wash the smell of kippers from his fingers. 'I have Bessie back, too, which is worth a lot to me. And I'd better get her home before the blizzard blocks my road.'

Jack stood up and followed him to the door. He would have gone with him, but Keithly stopped him. 'No. Don't you understand? This is your world now. You have to stay here.'

But it didn't feel at all like his world to Jack. As soon as Keithly was gone, he was collared by the housekeeper and ordered into the hottest and deepest bath he had ever taken. The water brought the circulation back into his fingers and toes far too fast, so that he moaned and whimpered with the pain. When it was finally over and he was beginning to relax and enjoy the fuggy warmth, it was time for him to come out and get dressed. The only clothes that could be found to fit him were cast-offs from the housekeeper's eleven-year-old son. The boots he was given to wear strangled his feet and made him feel clumsy as a carthorse. By the time he was fit to be presented in the drawing room he was in a state of acute embarrassment and had to be physically restrained from making a run for it.

The Duke and his wife were waiting for him. The largest fire that Jack had ever seen was blazing in the hearth. He could feel the heat from the doorway where he stood for a long minute before allowing himself to be coaxed nearer. He could not, however, be induced to sit on the upholstered armchair that was offered to him. Instead he stood in the middle of the room, shifting from one foot to the other and wringing his hands.

The housekeeper left. The gentlefolk looked at Jack long and hard. Finally, Lady Gordon sighed.

'You and your fine ideas,' she said. Jack glanced up, unsure whether or not he was being addressed, but the lady was facing her husband. Her eyes were red and puffy, as though she had been crying.

'I assumed that it would take a good horseman to catch the colt,' the Duke replied. 'I couldn't see any harm in having a good horseman in the family.'

'You couldn't see anything beyond getting your horse back and that's the truth.' Lady Gordon shook her head, still in a state of disbelief. 'You're going to have a fine time explaining this to Eleanor.'

Gordon groaned quietly. After a long pause, his wife sighed again. 'I suppose it could be worse,' she said.

'How?' said her husband.

'Well, at least he's young. Still malleable in body and mind. We might make something of him yet.'

Jack wondered if they considered him deaf. He felt a bit like a horse being offered for sale.

'You could be right,' said the Duke. 'And perhaps he does have the makings of a good horseman. If he were a bit stronger he might make a useful jockey.'

A hard stare from his wife silenced him. She turned to Jack, who dropped his eyes instinctively.

'How old are you?'

'Fourteen,' said Jack. 'Or no, maybe fifteen by now. I think I'm probably fifteen.'

'Don't you know?'

'Not exactly.'

'Well, when is your birthday?'

'My birthday?' said Jack, perplexed. 'But only little children have birthdays.'

Lady Gordon shook her head, bemused. 'No birthday? We shall have to give you one, then.' Her voice seemed a little brighter. 'I should enjoy that, I think. And what about your name?'

'Jack.'

'That won't do, either. We shall have to come up with a name for you as well as a birthday. Edwin, perhaps, or Edmund.'

'Cyril?' suggested her husband. 'Cedric?'

'Or James. James would suit him well, don't you think?' She clasped her hands in pleasure. 'In any case, we have plenty of time to work out the details and make a gentleman of him. Eleanor is still only fourteen and they are both too young to be married. We need to give them at least two years.

And by that time, things may look very different.'

'Very different indeed,' said the Duke. 'This is all quite splendid!' He smiled radiantly at his wife, with the air of a man who had just been let off a particularly nasty hook.

The sun still hadn't set on that same day when Jack found himself standing on the threshold of his new life. Behind him, a blizzard blew. In front of him, the wide, flagged hall of his own manor house invited him to enter and take possession of it. There were wolfhounds already in residence and in the tree-lined pastures surrounding the house, small groups of brood-mares huddled in sheltered corners, their tails to the bitter wind.

It was more than Jack had ever dared to wish for. He was to be like Master Gregory with his grand house, his servants, his fine horses. All this was to be his, and for nothing, it seemed, beyond taking Nell's advice and daring to dream.

The estate manager was still holding the door open. The housekeeper and two serving maids waited inside for Jack to acknowledge them. He could smell the smoke of blazing hearth-fires and the sweet aroma of roasting meat. All he had to do was to put one foot in front of the other and his previous cold, hungry existence would be behind him, shut out in the deepening snow. Why should it be so difficult?

The wind snatched at his hair. Never had the presence of Hermes seemed so close, or so real. Jack shivered, glanced back at the gathering dusk and stepped forward into his new life.

Chapter Seventeen

THAT night Jack slept poorly. His new circumstances were impossible for him to believe, and his mind was so confused by them that he lost the distinction between dreams and reality. Early the next morning, Jack and the estate manager, Adam Corbett, rode the four miles between Musgrave House and the manor in the landau. The day was cold and hazy and the horses' breath plumed around them, dampening Adam's jacket and the fine wool of the riding cape that the maid had laid out for Jack. As they passed the cottages of the Duke's tenants and labourers, women and children nodded solemnly to them and Jack did his best to hide his face inside the folds of his cloak.

When they arrived at the manor-house, Adam took the horses round to the stable yard. Jack stood uncertainly at the foot of the marble steps for a while, then lost his nerve and followed. The first thing he saw was the Arab colt looking out over his door.

There were voices in the tack room but no sign of any staff. Talking quietly as he had done that day in the marsh, Jack approached the young horse. He looked very different now. His chestnut coat gleamed from a thousand brush-strokes and his fine mane was without snarl or tangle. A proud light glinted in his clear, black eye.

Jack ran a hand down his delicate dished nose and patted his sleek, muscular neck, talking all the time. 'We're both captives now, lad, aren't we? Was I right to bring you here?'

The colt sniffed at Jack's fingers, his lips nibbling but never biting, then reached up and blew sweet breath into his face. Jack laughed and blew back. The colt nuzzled at his hair.

'My god,' came a soft voice from somewhere behind. 'Would you look at that.'

Jack turned round. The head groom was standing in the

middle of the yard, a look of amazement on his face. 'He remembers you,' he said.

'Of course he does,' said Jack, laughing again as the colt caught a fold of his sleeve and tugged gently at it.

'But you don't know,' said the groom. 'That horse is a demon to handle. We had the devil of a job to tidy him up. Took four of us to manage it. You wait there while I go and get his lordship.'

Jack waited willingly, rubbing the colt's forehead and letting him lick the salt from his hands. When the Duke arrived, he was as astonished as his groom.

'I wouldn't have believed it if I hadn't seen it,' he said.

'It's because the lad . . . Master James that is, pulled him out of the mire,' said the groom. 'They do remember, you know.'

The Duke nodded thoughtfully and a few minutes passed. The other stable boys gathered and watched from a distance. Finally the Duke seemed to reach a decision. He turned to the head groom.

'How would you like to go and live at Musgrave House?' he said.

'Me, sir? Why?'

'Because I intend for the colt to be kept there with James, at least for the time being. If we have a chance to put some manners on him we must take it, otherwise we'll be fighting with him for the rest of his life. Perhaps between the two of you, you can get his confidence.'

Jack was delighted with the idea, but his spirits rapidly diminished as the Duke led him into the house.

His betrothed was sitting in an armchair in the drawing room, her face turned towards the embroidered screen which protected her complexion from the direct heat of the fire. Her mother sat opposite and the Duke settled in beside her on the long couch. Jack was offered a second armchair, close beside Eleanor's. He sat down gingerly. She did not turn her head.

'Meet James, Eleanor,' said the Duke. Still she did not turn. Jack glanced at the side of her face. He tried not to stare, but from the beginning it was to be a losing battle. It wasn't that she was beautiful, although she probably was, in her own, indefinable sort of way. What struck Jack with a force that made him weak at the knee, was her resemblance to the White Queen in the picture on the alchemist's wall. The image imprinted itself afresh in his mind, all but obliterating the scene in the room in front of his eyes. The face of the queen was her face.

'Eleanor,' said her father again, a hint of admonition in his tone. 'Please say good morning to James.'

'Good morning, James.' Her voice was devoid of all feeling. She did not look at him.

'How do you do,' said Jack. His voice sounded as though it was struggling past a huge restriction. He did his best to clear the croak out of, then tried again. 'I'm very pleased to meet you.'

Lady Gordon stood up and walked across to her daughter. Gently but firmly she took her by the hand and drew her to her feet, then turned her round to face Jack. Her eyes were the palest blue and piercingly bright, but disdainful as those of the hawk that Jack had once seen watching him from a roadside branch.

He leapt to his feet, his fingers nervously twisting the lowest button of his waistcoat. Slowly, scornfully, Eleanor looked him up and down. He dropped his gaze to the floor, and when he found the courage to raise it again Eleanor had gone from him and was standing face to face with her father. In a voice that was gritty with rancour, she said, 'I hate you.'

'Eleanor!' said her mother, but the girl was not to be silenced.

'You love your horses more than you love me,' she said. With her head high and her back as stiff as a poker, she walked to the door and opened it. Then she threw a last, withering glance at Jack and said, 'I thought it was only in fairy tales that princesses were obliged to marry frogs!'

She was gone. Lady Gordon followed, a furious expression on her face. Her husband remained seated on the couch, his head in his hands. A dreadful silence fell. Eleanor might be the White Queen, but Jack was no longer the Red King, nor any other sort of dignitary. For an instant he wished he really was a frog, and could scuttle in behind the heap of logs beside the hearth.

'May I go, sir?' he found the courage to say.

The Duke seemed slightly surprised when he looked up, as though he had forgotten Jack was there.

'Yes, if you wish,' he said. 'You mustn't worry about my daughter, James. She is wilful, but she will come round, I promise. When the time comes, she will marry you.'

Chapter Eighteen

UNTIL that moment, the idea of marrying anyone had been so absurd to Jack that it hadn't even entered into his thinking. Before he met Eleanor, Jack had not been aware of any need for female companionship. But now, it seemed to him that his existence, despite the extraordinary changes in his circumstances, was incomplete without her. She became the most important thing in his life. It seemed to him, as he reflected on the events that had brought him to that place, that everything had been designed, by Hermes or some other instrument of fate, to bring him to Eleanor and her to him. But every time his thoughts ran along these lines, he came up against the same, unpalatable truth. Eleanor didn't feel the same way about him.

Over the next few days, Jack existed in a state of abject misery. He felt like an intruder in the huge house and skulked around the place, seeking out dark corners, trying to keep out of everybody's way. Even the dogs appeared to consider him unworthy of their attention and declined his offers of friendship with contempt.

Each morning, Adam Corbett took Jack out around the estate in an effort to familiarise him with his new responsibilities. Together they walked the forests and parklands and were driven in the carriage to outlying reaches of the land, where flocks of fat sheep were tended by shepherd boys who were introduced to Jack as their new employer. Jack tagged along unhappily, but took in little. His mind was fully occupied by images of Eleanor, and her words drowned out Adam's attempts to involve him in the running of the farm.

'. . . a frog . . . only in fairy tales . . . marry a frog.'

The turning point in Jack's attitude came one afternoon when

Adam took him to visit one of the tenant families in a remote, hilly area at the edge of the estate. The house was on the poorest of land, battered by the harsh weather, and the instant Jack set foot inside it he became profoundly uncomfortable. The unhappy dreams of Eleanor dispersed and he began to come to his senses.

The damp little cottage reminded him of his own origins; the sick child who lay on the settle bed beside the weak fire might have been one of his own dying brothers. The family offered Adam and Jack the best of their hospitality; a drop of precious rum from a dusty bottle kept on top of the dresser. It burned Jack's belly as he rapidly drank it down, eager to be finished and gone from that awful place with its uncomfortable reminders of unhappiness. Back outside in the carriage he waited for the more courteous Adam to rejoin him.

The rum added fire to his emotions. Life was the same everywhere. The poor suffered and died and there was nothing they could do about it. Their lives would never improve. Health and happiness were the prerogatives of the wealthy.

It was a full minute more before the truth dawned on Jack. He was no longer one of the struggling poor like the people beneath that leaking roof. He was one of the gentry.

When Adam came out again Jack, emboldened by the rum perhaps, had completed the mental shift into his new role. His voice shook slightly but it was, nonetheless, the voice of authority.

'Send the doctor out to that child,' he said. 'And collect no more rent from that family until he is better.'

Adam Corbett smiled. 'Very good, sir,' he said.

Jack was no longer a frog. He was a rich man. He was the Red King and the flames beneath his feet were already fuelling his determination to be all that his White Queen could wish for in a husband. When she saw him as he intended to be she would look upon him with amazement and delight. Like the figures in the picture they would turn towards each other and their lives together would be rapturous, a true union of souls. Musgrave House would ring to the sound of their delighted laughter and to the calls of the divine child that would be born to them.

What Jack failed to notice was how rapidly the satisfaction of one desire led to the birth of another. He was wealthy. All the needs he had been aware of could now be met; he would never have to be hungry again.

But instead of satisfaction, he had merely shifted his attention on to a new need. There was something else that he wanted.

Chapter Nineteen

On the morning of Jack's sixth day in residence, a small, portly man arrived by carriage at Musgrave Hall. He had with him a large number of cases and parcels of books tied with string which the servants proceeded to carry into the house. Jack stood inside the front door and tried to keep out of the way, but the newcomer bore down on him with an outstretched hand.

'Jacob Marley,' he said. 'And you are James?'

Jack nodded and took the small, pink hand. It was cool and damp and lay limp as a dead frog in his own. He let go of it hurriedly.

'I am to be your tutor,' said Marley. 'I will teach you to read and write and to comport yourself properly in good company.' He smiled slackly, and added, 'If it is possible.'

The following day, and every day afterwards, an instructor came to give Jack riding lessons. A second teacher turned up three times a week to teach him archery and falconry and Jack was soon so busy that he no longer had time to worry about the extraordinary changes in his circumstances.

A large part of every morning was given over to learning how to run the estate and look after the books. Before dinner and again afterwards, Marley drilled Jack with letters and numbers, grammar and pronunciation, manners and comportment and ethics. Any hours of daylight that were not taken up with outdoor activities seemed immediately to be filled by barbers or shoemakers, or by tailors coming to measure him for yet another suit of clothes. Every night he went to bed exhausted with the day's new knowledge circling his mind. Often he slept poorly because the rich food that the cook provided to build up his constitution disagreed with his digestive system. Then, just as he was beginning to get accustomed to that, the Duke came up with a new form of torture.

He appointed his personal surgeon to examine Jack's rickety legs and accompanied him on his first visit to Musgrave House. Once again Jack felt like an animal being inspected. He was required to take down his trousers while the surgeon poked and prodded and squeezed at his legs, sometimes quite painfully. When he had completed his examination he offered his opinions and suggestions to the Duke as though Jack wasn't present at all. Then, a few days later, he arrived with his solution. It was a pair of steel braces which he attached to Jack's legs with stout, leather straps. They exerted a strong, inward pressure on the bowed thighs and calves, causing immediate and severe discomfort. The surgeon assured Jack that it would all be worthwhile; that in time his legs would straighten if only he were resolute enough to wear the braces all the time except, of course, when riding.

It was almost more than Jack could bear. At night the pain brought tears to his eyes and banished any hope of sleep. He wondered what pleasure there could possibly be in having such wealth when the pressures of such an existence were so intolerable. But even at the worst of times the prospect of becoming the Red King and living in harmony with his partner sustained him. And when, in the quietest moments of the night, he thought of the alchemist, the memory of Barnstable's mischievous smile brought him some degree of comfort.

As time went by things began to improve for Jack. His legs and digestion adjusted to the new conditions and he began to get an appreciation for good food and comfortable living. He realised that the servants were, in fact, there to serve him and, timidly at first, he began to order things to suit himself. He did not want a fire in his bedroom; it made the place stuffy and gave him a headache. He preferred some foods to others. The dogs had accepted him now that he was the undisputed leader of the household, and he insisted that they be allowed to sleep on his bed at night and sit on the comfortable chairs in the drawing room. In addition, he wanted to take a walk on his own from time to time, with no questions asked.

During those walks he returned, in a limited way, to searching for the *prima materia*, slipping off the main paths of the estate into spinneys and ditches. When the condition of his clothes began to arouse suspicion, he asserted that he had an interest in relics and it was his privilege to search for them as he pleased. The staff accepted his eccentricity, as they accepted all eccentricities of the gentry, without question.

Jack's confidence began to grow, especially after he made an abrupt leap forward in his lessons with Marley. All those letters and words that had previously been nothing more than a cause of extreme anxiety suddenly took on meaning for him. The books on the library shelves were no longer forbidding monstrosities but friends waiting to make his acquaintance. Reading was still an enormous struggle and there were far more words in the language than Jack could ever have imagined, but one by one he was coming to know and appreciate them.

And if ever he grew tired or frustrated, dreams of his White Queen revitalised him. Although it was to be a long time before they met face to face again, Jack occasionally caught glimpses of Eleanor walking in the meadows and gardens around the manor or out riding on her light-boned hack. If she ever noticed him she gave no sign of recognition, but it didn't matter to Jack. Each sight of her added fuel to his dreams and his determination to prove himself worthy of her.

Tentatively at first but with growing courage, he questioned his staff about her. They were willing enough to share what they knew, and Jack's initial impressions of Eleanor were gradually augmented until he felt he knew her inside out. She was an excellent rider and a gifted musician; a bright, energetic character with an unbridled curiosity about the world. In general, he was told, she had a warm and outgoing temperament, but she could, at times, be wilful. If her heart was set on some course of action, no power on earth could turn her away from it. While he knew better than to criticize Lord Gordon's daughter, Marley contrived to suggest that this was not a commendable quality in a woman though why that should be, Jack wasn't sure. As far as he was concerned, Eleanor was perfect. If she was truculent and stubborn, then truculence and stubbornness were desirable qualities and Jack did his best to encourage them in himself. In trying to emulate her he went through a surprising change of character, becoming gradually calmer, more confident and outgoing in his manner, more assertive in his decisions. He would, he was certain, make himself a fitting partner for the girl he loved.

Chapter Twenty

Of all Jack's many pleasures on the Musgrave estate, the greatest was the chestnut colt. Under Jack's careful and patient guidance, he lost his mistrust of people and became mannerly and secure. Gradually, he filled out and grew into himself. Over the seasons that followed, he reached his full potential and Jack did too. They had the best of everything. Any deprivations their bodies might have suffered in their early years was made up for now. Jack grew like a summer weed on a compost heap, upwards first, several inches in a year, then outwards, bursting out of one set of clothes after another as his frame filled with muscular flesh. He was constantly active, out on his land day after day, learning the business from the estate manager, and getting on to first name terms with the tenants who farmed it. Any daylight hours that remained were devoted to sport; to archery and fencing and to hunting with hawk and hounds. The winter was long and there wasn't much of a spring, but the summer which followed was glorious and the long, hot days were filled with vigorous activity as Jack began to take his place in society. Although he was not entirely accepted by his peers among the county gentry, he worked hard to become their equal in the manly pursuits they employed. He ignored their occasional derision and refused to allow anything to undermine his determination. And it worked. The more he ran and rode and swam, the stronger his body became and the healthier his appetite. He grew so rapidly that, before the summer was out, a new set of braces had to be made for him. He buckled them up to their limit every night and learned to sleep despite the discomfort. Slowly but surely they were bringing about the desired effect. Jack grew fit and healthy.

And wealthy. Jack had no formal education, but he lacked nothing in intelligence. The estate had always run well, even in the absence of a resident owner, and before his first year as its manager was over, Jack had learned how to improve it further. With the help of Adam Corbett he turned the estate into a hugely successful enterprise. He treated his tenants and farm labourers well, and they worked well for him in return. He cleared a hundred acres of scrubland and used the cleared area for intensive beef production, employing extra men to tend the expanding herd. He used his eye for horseflesh to great advantage, attending every sale within reach, buying run-down animals and turning them out on his meadows to improve, then schooling them and selling them on at a profit.

To begin with, Neville Gordon kept a tight hand on Jack's finances. Until he married Eleanor, the estate didn't belong to Jack and he was merely learning about its operation while he waited for Eleanor to come of age. But as time went by and he saw that Jack was efficient and trustworthy, Gordon relaxed his grip and the Musgrave money remained at the house, in a strongbox in the office. Adam Corbett was uneasy about its presence there, but Jack had a poor man's mistrust of financial institutions and refused to have anything to do with banks or bonds. The money he acquired stayed where he could see it and feel it and count it.

Educationally, as well, Jack was accumulating merit. Marley, aloof and disdainful to begin with, could not fail to be impressed by Jack's energy and hard work. He discovered in himself a renewed enthusiasm for teaching and moved Jack rapidly through the available English texts. When the days shortened and the year turned towards winter again, they took up the study of mathematics and science and of Latin and Greek, and Jack was required to read extensively around his subjects. It was during this time that he arrived, for the first time, at a reference to Hermes.

It shocked him so much that Marley, who was sitting with him over the translation of the text, thought that he had taken a seizure.

'Are you all right, James?'

'Yes, I'm fine. I just . . . felt a little dizzy, that's all.'

'Perhaps I'm working you too hard. Do we need better light? Put your head down between your knees for a while. That always helps.'

Jack did so, glad of the respite. His mind was still reeling. He had kept his experience with the alchemist so private that it was like part of his soul, and to find that Hermes had an existence outside the secret fraternity was like a discovery of betrayal. Marley patted him on the back with limpid concern, and gradually his curiosity overcame his shock. He sat up straight again and returned to the text.

'Where were we?' he said.

'Are you sure you're all right?'

'Quite sure. Here we are. Zeus and Hermes. Who was Hermes, exactly?'

Marley's face took on an unexpected enthusiasm. 'Ah,' he said, 'I'm glad you asked me that. Hermes was not the greatest of the Greek gods, but he was certainly the most interesting. Zeus was his father, but his mother was a mortal, which gave him the ability to move easily between Mount Olympus and the world of mortals. Because of this, he was appointed messenger of the gods. He was also the escort of souls on their last journey into the underworld.'

Jack shuddered perceptibly and Marley looked at him with an anxious expression. 'Are you sure you are well?'

'Yes, yes,' said Jack. 'Please go on.'

'Well, Hermes was also the god of travellers, and of thieves and tricksters, that sort of thing. In fact, his first exploit in life was to steal Apollo's cattle from him,' Marley went on, but Jack heard no more. He was lost in the memory of his own first theft, and how he had attributed it to Hermes without any knowledge of what he was doing. For the first time in more than a year he became aware of the capricious presence hovering in the air around him, and for a while he was lost to enthralment. When he became conscious of Marley again, he was still talking.

'The Romans called him Mercury, and the elusive quicksilver was named after him. That is probably the reason that he was adopted by the alchemists as their divinity . . .'

Jack interrupted him. 'Alchemists? What do you know about alchemists?' His voice had an uncharacteristic urgency about it and Marley stared at him with growing concern.

'Perhaps you might prefer to rest for a while, James? We could continue with this tomorrow.'

Jack took a deep breath and got a grip on himself. 'No,' he said, adopting a more diffident air. 'I was just curious, that's all. What on earth is an alchemist, anyway?'

Marley observed his pupil warily for a moment, but eventually continued. 'Alchemists, yes. I think the best way of describing it to you, James, is as a sort of madness.'

'Madness? What do you mean?'

'There are no alchemists any longer. The practice was banned during the last century, and with good reason.'

'Oh?'

'Yes. The foolish practitioners of this science believed that by following certain rather ritualistic procedures, they could turn base metals into gold.' He gave a short, patronising laugh, which Jack tried unsuccessfully to mimic. 'Absurd, of course,' he went on. 'There is no such procedure.'

'I suppose not,' said Jack.

'No. There are other theories, of course. It has been proposed that making gold was never the purpose of the exercise, that it was, rather, a philosophy of the spirit.'

'In what sense?'

'Well, it is only a theory, and a somewhat preposterous one at that, but it is said that the alchemists' references to gold were purely symbolic. They made much of the Red King and the White Queen, equivalent to red sulphur and white lead, which are supposed to do a good deal of chasing around together in the chemical fermentation and eventually combine to make gold. But the proponents of the theory of spirit claim that this Red King and White Queen represent the male and female aspects of the alchemist himself, which must be brought to union within his soul, thus producing an offspring; the divine child. Otherwise known as immortality.'

Jack gaped in bewilderment. Marley laughed, quietly. 'You are quite lost, I see. And so you should be. It is all so much nonsense and there is, in my opinion, only one definition of alchemy.'

'And that is?'

'I have already told you. It is a form of madness.' He smiled, clearly enchanted by his own erudition. 'You see, James' he went on in a paternal tone, 'it is now well known that quicksilver is highly poisonous. These alchemist chappies spent all their days locked up in stuffy little workshops refining mercury from cinnabar and mixing it with all kinds of noxious things. It is no wonder that they became mad. They were poisoned by the fumes, you see, which created delusions and hallucinations. Their writings are proof of this, apparently, though I have never seen them myself.'

He stopped, and for a while they sat in silence. Jack sent out feelers, hoping to find the presence of Hermes around him in the air, but the wind which rattled the shutters carried nothing more mysterious than rain. Jack felt a dreadful gloom descend upon the room and upon his life. 'I think I will take that rest, after all,' he said.

That night Jack lay awake for a long time, revising his memories in accordance with what he had been told. Marley, with his piles of books and his massive knowledge of languages, science and mathematics, had to be right. In Jack's mind, the alchemist's face lost its previous charm. His gentle smile became a foolish grin; the mischievous glint in the eyes proof of insanity. His own belief in Hermes became frightening to him, a sign, perhaps, of some incipient madness that the alchemist had seeded, and he resolved to dismiss it from his mind and not think of it again. The only thing that sustained him through those bleak hours was the image of the Red King and the White Queen. They had to be real; their union had to come about. To even conceive that it might not happen would have been more than Jack could bear.

A few days later, Jack received a summons from the manor to call around in the afternoon. Still shaken by the sudden revision of his beliefs, Jack was unnerved by the prospect of a visit with Lord Gordon, and the remote, but nonetheless daunting prospect that he might catch a glimpse of Eleanor.

The little cob, still Jack's favourite, jogged along jauntily, happy to be out with the wind blowing through his tail, but Jack didn't enjoy the ride at all. He was cold, not from the wind, but from some numbness within. There was an ominous feeling about the day which, since he could no longer attribute such things to Hermes, Jack was doing his best to dismiss. But he was having little success.

At the manor, the Duke's mood seemed to match his own. The huge drawing room resounded with emptiness. Jack and the Duke were like strangers passing through it. They sat for some time in uneasy silence, and Jack found himself wondering whether some awful catastrophe had befallen them all. But eventually Lord Gordon ran a hand through his iron-grey hair and sighed.

'I have to tell you, James, that all my efforts at persuasion have been without success. I had hoped to have good news for you today but Eleanor, I'm afraid, has still not resigned herself to this match.' He stood up and walked over to the fire, which was roaring more furiously than ever as the high winds dragged at the chimney. 'I'm afraid I have wasted your time in fetching you here.'

Chapter Twenty-one

JACK should have seen the truth then and realised the difference between fantasy and reality. But the Red King and the White Queen exerted such a powerful force in his imagination that he couldn't even contemplate the possibility that they would not come together and complete the roles he had assigned to them. At night he had disturbing dreams; of marriages forced at sword-point, and of Eleanor weeping inconsolably; but he preferred to ignore the messages they were giving him and hold on to his hopes.

But something had changed. Despite himself, Jack had lost his newfound assurance, and his underlying insecurities began to emerge in new and destructive forms. Outwardly, he continued to function much as he had before, but there were subtle changes that began to make themselves evident in the weeks and months that followed. The first was that Jack's appetite began to get out of control. The good food that had been so necessary for his undernourished body lost its taste for him. Nothing would please him but the youngest, tenderest lamb and pork, the richest sauces, the sweetest cakes and puddings. Twice a day he sat down to meals of seven or eight courses, and in between he would often call the cook or the housekeeper to serve him up some delicacy in the drawing room.

He got no exercise, other than the occasional ride around his property on the Arab colt, and his studies all but came to an end. He began to grow fat, but although he hated this manifestation of his gluttony, he didn't hate it enough to put an end to it. As long as he wasn't too heavy for the colt, he could see no reason to stop indulging himself.

The worst casualty of his excesses, however, was not himself, but the estate. With the assistance of Adam Corbett, Jack had managed the property brilliantly. Relations with the tenants were healthy and the land was producing good crops, good stock, and good hunting. But with Jack's new priorities, all that changed. He was no longer interested in efficient management; merely in profit. He examined the books and raised the rents. He increased the stocking levels on the land in order to have more sheep and cattle to sell. Worst of all, perhaps, he felled a huge acreage of ancient oaks, sold the trees to a ship-builder and ordered the land to be cleared for yet more grazing stock.

Adam Corbett did his best to curb the destruction, but Jack was beyond control. His strong-box was filling rapidly and, despite the fact that the increased wealth brought him neither happiness nor security, he continued in his determination to make more of it.

Nothing was denied him. He became whimsical in his demands, making life difficult for his domestic staff, who were kept on the run constantly, bringing him this and that. The more tyrannical he grew, the more certain he became that there was nothing on earth that he couldn't have if he desired it. And it was this belief that finally brought an end to the destruction.

One morning in May, Jack sent a messenger to the manor to say that he intended to meet with Mistress Eleanor and would arrive in the early afternoon. For what remained of the morning, he preened himself in front of his mirror, trying one wig, one top-coat after another, tormenting his manservant with capricious demands for powder and beauty-spots which never quite succeeded in pleasing him. Time, rather than satisfaction, eventually brought the process to an end, and Jack set out in the landau to meet his bride to be and to finalise the matter of their wedding day.

Neither Lord nor Lady Gordon were in evidence, but Jack attributed no significance to the fact. He followed the housekeeper to the drawing room and sat down to wait until Eleanor arrived. It never occurred to him that she wouldn't and he happened to be right. Within five minutes she appeared in the doorway and came into the room.

Jack rose to his feet and dipped his head in a formal bow. Eleanor had matured since he had last seen her and the pale blue, almost white gown that she wore hung gracefully around curves that had not been there before. With complete self-assurance she crossed the room and sat down, to Jack's surprise, in the chair nearest to his. Her eyes were still the same, delicate blue, but the expression in them was quite different from the one they had worn on the last occasion.

Jack's hopes were resurrected. More than ever, Eleanor resembled the White Queen, and the impoverished images that he had worked so hard to preserve filled out and became substantial again. But Eleanor's feelings were not in accord with his own.

'Poor James,' she said. 'I'm afraid that you are an innocent victim in all of this mess.'

Her kindness disarmed Jack more thoroughly than any hostility could have done. His confident manner evaporated. He was as shy before her as he had been on their first meeting. And that old, small Jack could not bear to hear the contrived name on her lips. In his dreams, she had never used it.

'It's not James, Eleanor,' he found himself saying. 'It's Jack.'

'Is it? Jack, then. I like that better than James. It suits you. But it makes no difference.'

'I suppose it doesn't.'

'No. You see, this conflict doesn't really concern you at all. I don't even know you, so how can I say whether or not I want to marry you?'

Jack felt hopeful. 'That can be mended,' he said. 'We can meet as often as you like.'

'I'm afraid not. This argument is between me and my father. I'm sorry if it causes you suffering, but it can't be helped. I will not marry you, James, not because of what you may or may not be, but because I will not allow my father to give me away in exchange for a horse.'

'It's not like that,' said Jack, but Eleanor continued speaking.

'If and when I marry, I shall marry the man of my choice

and not one chosen for me, whatever reason might be given.'

'Choose me, then,' said Jack. 'You could find plenty of men with worse prospects after all.'

A silence fell between them which Jack found himself unable to breach. The flames made occasional gigantic leaps for the chimney as though they were trying to escape the solemn atmosphere, but the Red King's fire was out, and Jack was lost for inspiration. A small, black beetle wandered aimlessly around the floor. Jack watched it, wishing he could think of something to say; it wouldn't matter what, as long as it relieved the appalling tension. But his mind and his heart were both quite empty. It was Eleanor who eventually spoke.

'I really am sorry, James.'

'Jack.'

'Jack. I have nothing against you at all. But I'll never marry you.'

In a sudden tide of anger, Jack's spoilt nature got the upper hand. In the imperious tones he had taken to using with his domestic staff, he said, 'You'll have to marry me, Eleanor. The fact of the matter is that you have no choice. It's an arrangement that your father and I have. You will become my wife, whether you want to or not.'

But if Jack expected the kind of response he generally got from his browbeaten servants, he was badly disappointed. Eleanor didn't even flinch, but looked steadily into his eyes.

'I will not be forced into this, by you or my father. If I have to, I shall end up like my aunt.'

'Your aunt? What aunt?'

Eleanor looked amazed. 'But surely you know about my aunt,' she said. 'It's her house you are living in, after all.'

'I thought it was yours,' he said.

'Well it is, in a way. At least it would be if I married you. But strictly speaking it still belongs to my aunt. She ran off with some farm boy or something, just as I will if I have to, because she wouldn't submit to the marriage my grandfather had arranged for her. When he died he left Musgrave House in trust for her in case she came back. But she never did. My father decided that it was time to give up on her. He says that she must surely be dead by now. And that's how her estate came to be set aside for me and whoever I should marry.' A shrewd grin came over her face as she spoke. 'But he should have known better than to give me her name.'

'Her name?' said Jack. 'She had the same name as you?'

Eleanor nodded, still smiling. 'She did. Although everyone knew her as Nell.'

The shock that ran through Jack's heart drove the last of his arrogance underground. Around him the air seemed to wobble, and without knowing what he was doing he stood up, grasping the arm of his chair for balance. How had she given it up? How could anyone choose to live in a miserable, damp cottage in a dreary little town when they could have all this? Why should it matter who you were married to?

'Are you all right?' There was genuine concern on Eleanor's lovely face. 'Should I ring for someone?'

'No,' said Jack, straightening himself up. 'But I have taken up quite enough of your time. I must get home before nightfall.'

'But it's not late, yet. You have plenty of time. Are you sure you're not ill?'

'Yes, I'm quite sure. Perhaps we might meet again some time?'

Before Eleanor had time to reply he had gone, crossing the room with improper haste and blundering through the kitchen to the stable yard where his solid little cob was patiently waiting. As he rode down the avenue, Jack tried to revive some last vestige of hope but it was no good. There was no denying the truth. The reminder of Nell's circumstances had finalised the matter in Jack's mind.There would be no wedding to Eleanor.

Chapter Twenty-two

BACK at Musgrave Hall, Jack rampaged through the house, dragging the servants and stable boys from their work or waking them from their naps, frightening the wits out of Marley who was reading beside the fire in the study.

'Out!' Jack yelled at them. 'I want you all out, now!'

Any of them that dared to ask questions were ignored or berated. Within minutes the house and buildings were empty and Jack was alone in the house that had once belonged, still belonged, to one of the only people in his life who had befriended him.

He ate his way through the larger part of a fruit cake and drank half a bottle of wine but they did nothing to comfort him. Life was putrid. There was no sense in expecting it to be otherwise. He had been foolish enough to believe that he might find acceptance in the world, but it wasn't so. They were all using him in one way or another; Lord Gordon, his wife, his daughter; not one of them cared about him in the slightest. Even Keithly, he reflected bitterly, had only delivered him to Gordon as a way of getting his revenge. He was still a frog. He would never be anything else. But he would not play along with their games. And no other innocent victim would ever be put through a similar torment. Not if he could help it.

He was haunted by Eleanor's face and the anguish of his rejected feelings for her. How could she treat him like that, after all he had been through for her? Life was rotten at the heart, like the egg that should have saved Matty.

The egg. He saw it again in his mother's hand. A plain, brown egg. It looked so innocent and full of promise, yet it contained only foulness. He knew it wasn't rational, but he held Barnstable directly responsible for all that had happened and he cursed the mad old fool and regretted the day he first met him.

It was past feeding time. A dozen eager heads appeared over their half doors when Jack walked into the stable yard. But the horses were to get no feeds that night. Instead, Jack went round the yard and opened the stable doors. The hunters, the brood mares, the carriage horses came out one by one and shifted around on the cobbles, touching noses enquiringly. The stallion watched, tossing his head and whickering with impatience, affronted at not being included in the mass liberation. Jack ignored him, and quietly shooed the whole herd out through the gate into the parkland. For a while he stood and watched them. He would miss them all, particularly the little cob. He might have stayed there even longer, taking that quiet leave, if the smell of burning timbers hadn't wafted through the night air and reminded him of what he was doing. But his movements were still unhurried as he closed the paddock gate and crossed the yard to open the ones which led on to the avenue.

The colt pricked his ears and sniffed the night with curiosity as Jack tacked him up and led him out into the yard. He was restless with excitement and wouldn't stand still, but it didn't matter to Jack who, despite the considerable extra weight of his full pockets and his money bags, sprang up on to his back as he was moving. The colt froze at the unaccustomed load, then dropped his head and propped a few strides on stiff legs. Jack sat tight and spoke to him calmly until he came to a halt, then dug his heels in hard and hissed as loud as he could. The colt sprang forward, propped again, then shot off through the open gates and into the darkness.

Behind them, the fire that Jack had set in Musgrave Hall was already sending flames leaping towards the stars.

Chapter Twenty-three

JACK rode quietly, going with the movements of the horse as naturally as possible. The night parted before them and flowed in their wake like dark water. To his surprise, Jack began to enjoy himself. He had never ridden the Arab at top speed, preferring always to keep him quiet and steady. Now he discovered that the colt's gait was not only faster than any he had experienced; it was smoother as well. He seemed to glide over the ground as though it offered him no resistance and despite the darkness he never once faltered or stumbled. One or two people, walking home late, scattered out of their path with expressions of terror. Jack grinned with delight and goaded the colt on, thrilled by the reckless race through the darkness. The only interference he made in their progress was to pull on the left rein occasionally, turning the horse's head towards the uplands and the moors beyond.

But it could not go on for long. The young horse was strong and healthy, but he was not fit. By the time they had covered two or three miles he slowed to a canter and finally, blowing hard, stopped. Jack slipped off him and led him onwards, up the steepening tracks. The higher they climbed, the smaller the fields became and the poorer the land they contained. After another mile or so, they rose over the lip of the horizon and Jack saw ahead of them, on the other side of the next vale, the grim expanse of the moors. If the colt saw them, too, he gave no sign, but followed Jack with a trust he was not sure he deserved.

They carried on across the mean, hungry land, where cottages which had once looked cosy and inviting to Jack now spoke of remembered poverty. In their dark interiors, children cried and coughed. More than once he thought of changing his mind, of trying to reclaim the oblivious comfort of the last two years. But he had burned his bridges along with his belongings and there was no turning back.

Throughout the night Jack and the colt walked across the moors. All kinds of sombre thoughts troubled Jack's mind, but it wasn't until dawn began to break that he realised just how rash and foolish his action had been. He had no regrets about setting fire to the house. It was a fitting end to the whole sorry mess of forced marriages and unhappy lives. But what he had not considered well enough was his escape. Jack owned the house, and could do what he liked with it. But he did not own the horse, and the word would soon be out that he had been stolen. With his fine bones and striking Arab features he would stand out like an escaped pachyderm, and there would be no way in the world to hide or disguise him.

So, as the sun rose above the skyline, Jack came to a decision. In every direction, the moors stretched relentlessly on. There wasn't a house or a wall to be seen. It was perfect. He put his arms around the colt's taut neck and clung to him for a moment. Then he slipped off the tack and swung the bridle around his head. The horse wheeled around in surprise, and Jack aimed a stinging blow at his rump, sending him bounding away across the rough ground. He did not, however, go far, but soon stopped and looked back.

Tears threatened Jack's resolve. He had more affinity with the colt than with any other living being, yet now, he realised, he was betraying him, using him as he himself had been used, to get revenge upon someone else. Three times he chased the horse off and walked away. Three times he followed and caught up with him again, but at last, the colt grew tired of the game. He wandered off with his nose to the ground, looking for something decent to eat among the rough vegetation. By the time he was ready to play again, Jack was long gone.

As he increased the distance between them, Jack knew that the horse would be found again, sooner or later. But this time, he was certain, the reward would not be a duke's daughter.

Chapter Twenty-four

It was late summer and the fruit in Jonathan Barnstable's garden was beginning to ripen, watched over by a new generation of straw people and animals. Chickens scratched beneath the trees and made dust baths for themselves in the shade. The alchemist sat beside his front door, soaking up the evening sun. A stray breeze ran like silky fingers through his grey hair and he straightened up, looking around him.

A young man appeared on the track and stood for a long time at the wicket gate, as though undecided. Barnstable stroked the small tabby cat which lay curled up on his lap and waited. Finally, the young man looked up in his direction and, seeing him, kicked the gate open and advanced up the path. The alchemist stayed quite still, watching. The youth's approach was energetic and belligerent. He did not stop until he was on the doorstep, looming over the older man.

'Good evening, Jack.' The cat poured out through the alchemist's hands like mottled sand and disappeared around the corner of the house.

'Good evening to you, too.' Jack shoved aside the straggling hair which flopped over his face, revealing a pair of hard, blue eyes.

'Welcome.' Barnstable stood up and extended a rough, square hand, but Jack declined to take it. Instead he glanced voraciously around the garden, fixing upon a sleepy chicken here, a plump cabbage there.

'Still doing well for yourself, I see.'

'Of course,' said the alchemist. 'Why should you expect otherwise?'

'Because it's better than you deserve,' said Jack. His tone was snide as he continued. 'I wonder how many innocent young lads you sent off on fools' errands like me. Hm? To break their hearts searching for something that doesn't exist?'

Barnstable laughed and Jack's eyes blazed with sudden anger. 'I suppose the country is littered with them, is it? Digging and poking and getting themselves covered with muck. And all for nothing.'

At the corner of the house the cat had reappeared and was glaring at Jack pugnaciously. Its keeper, however, was quite calm.

'No, no, Jack,' he said. 'You are quite wrong. I have only taken on one apprentice, and that is you.'

Jack laughed derisively. 'You really are mad, old man. I am not your apprentice, nor was I. I was a poor, gullible boy, deluded by the promise of gold. But never, I'm glad to say, as deluded as you are.'

Barnstable smiled to himself and gazed for a few moments into the middle distance. Then he sighed and stood up, looking searchingly at Jack.

'Tell me about delusion,' he said.

Jack took an involuntary step backwards. The alchemist's eyes held such brilliant intensity that he couldn't look at them, and his antagonism evaporated despite his determination to hold on to it.

'You have come a long way, Jack,' Barnstable went on. 'Great changes have taken place in you since we last met. You seem to have found rather a good tailor, though your clothes have clearly seen better days. Even your voice has changed. You have become quite the young gentleman, and I imagine that you have received a substantial education somewhere or other. Am I right?'

Jack nodded sulkily. He felt like a child again beneath the powerful gaze. The cat relaxed its aggressive stance and began to lick its belly.

'So tell me about delusion,' said the alchemist.

Someone must have drugged him at the inn in Shipley where he put up for the night. He remembered nothing beyond the meal and the drink downstairs. He didn't know whether he ever made it to bed, or whether he wandered, or was led, out into the night, through the narrow streets and out into the countryside beyond. That was where he had woken, lying by the side of the road with an excruciating headache.

It was some time before he understood what had happened. When he succeeded in getting to his feet, his pockets felt as heavy as they had since he left Musgrave Hall. But he hadn't gone a hundred paces down the road before he knew, with gut-wrenching certainty, that it wasn't his money that was weighing him down.

Every bag, every pocket in his clothes was filled with stones. Jack sat down in the road, too numb even to weep. A light breeze rustled the leaves above his head, and in it he began to hear a familiar voice; feel a familiar presence. Hermes was back, and would not be ignored. Long before Jack got up and set out again, he knew that there was only one place now that he could go.

As he walked along the leafy lanes, he left an irregular line of stones in his wake, like a trail for the despairing to follow.

'Tell me about delusion.'

It wasn't the wealth that had been a delusion. That had been real enough and the power that went with it. It was his thinking that had been wrong; the belief that he could have whatever he wanted, and that having whatever he wanted would make him happy. He had experienced pleasures of the mind and body at Musgrave Hall, but none of them had satisfied his soul.

The alchemist waited, and then, since Jack seemed unable to summon a response, he went on. 'Never mind. We have plenty of time to discuss these things. What matters is that you are back.'

Jack's anger returned like a rush of blood. 'Back! I'm not back! Why should I want to come back? To poison myself with mercury fumes like you? So that I can end up as mad as you are?'

Barnstable laughed so forcibly that the chickens paused in their scratching and looked around in alarm. He laughed so long and so hard that he had to sit down again and wipe the tears from his eyes. Jack's fury seemed to rise in direct proportion to the other's mirth.

'That proves it!' he shouted. 'Look at you. Look at you. You're a lunatic. You should be locked up!'

The alchemist recovered himself at last and looked up. 'Dear Jack,' he said. 'You are back, you know, and I am very glad to see you.'

Jack felt his heart rising to meet the affection which sparkled in Barnstable's gaze. He fought it down again. 'I'm not back!'

'Then why are you here?'

'I'm here because . . . because . . .' He found he couldn't remember, though he was sure that there had been some sane and valid reason. 'I'm here to get some of that gold you claim to have made,' he finished lamely. 'You owe me that at least, after all the trouble you've caused me.'

'You shall have it, of course. But I'm afraid you will have to make it yourself this time.'

Jack shook his head furiously. 'There you are. You're already trying to trick me again.'

The alchemist stifled another laugh. 'I have no intention of tricking you, none at all. But you have returned to me, Jack. What's more, unless I am mistaken, you have achieved what you set out to do.'

Jack was flabbergasted. 'What? Found your stupid old black stuff? You must be joking.'

'I'm not joking. And you do have the stupid old black stuff. I can see it in your face.'

'You really are mad,' said Jack. 'I have nothing, can't you see that? Nothing at all. And I don't want to hear any more of your nonsense.' He turned and began to walk away down the path.

'Empty out your pockets, Jack.'

Something in Barnstable's tone made him stop and turn back. 'They're empty.'

'Turn them out, anyway.'

Jack gritted his teeth and dragged the linings out of his trouser pockets. 'Satisfied now? Nothing but holes.'

'Your waistcoat.'

With a disdainful expression Jack thrust his thumb and forefinger into his small breast pocket. He stopped, staring at the alchemist with disbelief. There was, after all, something there. He had known it was there. It had been there for weeks, a small bulge in his pocket, familiar as a part of himself. He pulled it out and laid it on the palm of his hand. One last stone, left by the person or people who had robbed him. One that he had missed when he emptied the rest out of his pockets.

'See? It's nothing. Just an old stone.' But even as he spoke, remembering how it had got there, he was anticipating Barnstable's response.

'That's it, though, isn't it? The *prima materia.* Matter born of darkness, all that is left of your dreams and aspirations.' The words touched off nerves in Jack's spine and sent tingles through his limbs. 'You forgot, perhaps, but your soul did not. You were searching whether you knew it or not, and eventually you found what you were looking for.'

'Are you trying to tell me I was looking for this? That I wanted to lose everything I had? That I had some choice in the matter?'

'Didn't you?'

While Jack struggled to find an answer, the alchemist went on, 'What matters isn't the choices we made or didn't make, Jack. What matters is the one that faces us now, and then the next one, and the next. Don't live in regret. Live in enthusiasm.'

'Enthusiasm?'

'Every day is a new adventure. And for you, the greatest adventure is waiting. If you choose to embark upon it.'

Jack stared at the plain little stone in his hand. What he couldn't understand was how he had carried it for so long without ever thinking about it. If he had, he would certainly have thrown it away. It was just a stone and yet, as Jack continued to stare at it, he knew that it wasn't. Like the alchemist himself, it possessed an extra quality that could not be defined. Something augmented it. It was more than itself.

Jack was trembling. His voice shook. 'There's no adventure. It's just a stone. A wretched little stone.'

'Throw it away, then. Continue along your way.'

The sun descended below the horizon and the chickens, with one mind, began to wander towards their perches. In the orchard, an apple dropped with a gentle thump into the dusty hollow that one of them had just vacated. The cat entwined herself around the alchemist's feet, describing the symbol of eternity.

Jack looked back the way he had come, then up into the alchemist's face. Slowly, still trembling slightly, he replaced the stone in his pocket.

Chapter Twenty-five

So, still not quite sure how it came about, Jack found himself living in the little cottage on the banks of the Thames with the alchemist. They shared the gardening and the cooking and the care of the chickens, but these things took up relatively little of their time. The bulk of it was given over to the study, both practical and theoretical, of alchemy.

Jack submitted to the tortuous routine of chemistry and reading without any clear sense of why he was doing it. In conversation with the alchemist he remained entirely sceptical; questioning everything he was taught and scoffing at the notion that it was possible to make gold in a bottle. In the quiet of his own thoughts he consistently told himself the same thing, but he could not dislodge the grain of hope that accompanied him, like that last little stone, in everything he did. It was all that kept him going; a small but significant counterweight to the bitterness that lay waiting to consume him during every lull in his routine. No matter how hard he tried he could not forget Eleanor, or put the humiliation of her rejection of him into the past.

The hours of daylight were largely spent in the laboratory. The first and most frequently repeated lessons concerned the treatment of the fires, with much attention being given to the art of draught control. The ovens and flues were fitted with an assortment of screws and dampers which regulated the amount of air reaching the fire and being pulled up the chimneys. Jack had to learn the uses of these down to the minutest detail, and the alchemist was ruthless in his demand for perfection.

Jack concentrated hard, and when Barnstable began to be satisfied with his development he allowed him to progress to the chemical side of the work. Gradually, over the months which followed, he learnt how to conduct simple chemical processes. He learnt how to refine and separate, distil and purify, combine and smelt and concentrate. He became familiar with vitriols and chlorides and alum, with phosphorous and sulphur, arsenic and ammonia, with tin and copper and lead and finally, reverentially, with the dangerous and elusive mercury.

'Mercury can indeed drive you mad,' Barnstable told him, 'but he will not if you learn to treat him with respect.' He showed Jack the large, permanent crucible where the liquid metal was refined from its ore, cinnabar. 'Once this is closed and sealed, no fumes can leak out into the room. They go straight up into the sky, do you see?'

Jack nodded, studying the broad flue that disappeared into the rafters.

'Only puffers need have fear of him,' Barnstable went on, 'and I do not think you are a puffer, Jack. I do not think there is any danger that you will go mad.'

Indeed, the more he saw of the alchemist, the harder it was to entertain the slightest possibility that he was insane, but nevertheless, Jack refused to relinquish the idea. He kept a close watch on his own behaviour in case some subtle manifestations of madness should begin to appear, and kept a journal in which he recorded his progress and his impressions, reading it back to himself from time to time, just to be safe. But for all his systematic logic, there were things that he could neither explain nor deny.

Like the time, one morning, when Jack saw the alchemist catch an apple falling from one of the trees in the orchard. Afterwards, he couldn't work out whether Barnstable had put out his hand before the apple began to drop or whether he had somehow sensed that it was falling and reached out in time to catch it. In either event, it was an extraordinary achievement; but although Jack was left staring in astonishment, the alchemist seemed to think nothing of it. He simply carried on strolling through the orchard, eating the apple as he went.

That occurrence, and others like it, brought the image of the divine child; the reborn Hermes, into Jack's mind. Although Barnstable rarely mentioned it, his words returned to Jack with regularity. 'But which matters more? Gold in the hand or gold in the spirit?'

Despite his innate resistance, Jack's mind was beginning to open to the unknown. Every night, surrounded by candles, he sat up late, working his way through Barnstable's library of esoteric texts. Some of them were so old that their pages crumbled as he turned them, and he had to squint and struggle over their faded lettering. Others were fresher, immaculately copied by steady hands and bound between strong covers. It made little difference to Jack; in the end one was as incomprehensible as the next. Some of them seemed to be fables, with metals or chemical substances as the leading characters instead of people. Others consisted of little more than lists of strange symbols, or drawings; the familiar snakes and dragons and lions; or alchemists from different civilizations going through their workshop routines; or series of pictures of what happened inside the sacred vessel. The most common theme, though, was that of the Red King and the White Queen. Jack came across their story in a number of different forms, sometimes illustrated, sometimes not. There were, however, certain elements common to them all. The king and queen were always watched over by Hermes. They emerged from a pool of water or embraced within it. Sometimes they merged into one and became a genderless being, or the small, radiant, Hermes child, and sometimes the child was the offspring of their marriage. The royal pair haunted Jack, reminding him persistently of his failure, embarrassing him by the foolishness of the dreams he had dared to dream and creating a great melancholy within him, stirred by memories of having loved and been rejected. But at times, they did more than that. In the early hours, when the presence of Hermes was at its strongest in the moving shadows cast by the candles, the stories inspired a sense of wonder, a realisation that they spoke of things which had no substance in the actual world, but existed nevertheless within the human soul. In the mornings, in the cold light of logic, these perceptions seemed absurd and he attributed them to tiredness and overwork. But as time went on and the number of similar experiences began to take up more space in his journal, he found that he could not so readily dismiss them. More and more often, his fingers would stray to the little bulge in his waistcoat pocket; his own *prima materia*, waiting to be processed.

It was just a stone, he kept telling himself, just a stone.

One night, early in March, the alchemist brought Jack out beneath a clear sky and showed him how to recognise certain of the planets and constellations.

'There may not be time to teach you how to measure their positions and work out their auspices,' he said, 'but it is not so urgent. This I can do for you, but nothing else.'

With the use of the strangest tools Jack had ever seen, Barnstable proceeded to take readings and measurements from things that could barely be seen, way above in the clear sky. It seemed to take forever and Jack grew cold standing there in the frosty grass of the garden. Eventually, when the alchemist was satisfied, they moved back into the house where the fire still glowed brightly.

'The timing of the Great Work is all-important,' said Barnstable, dropping to his knees beside a pile of charts and almanacs. Jack settled down beside him and watched as, with painstaking care, he drew up a new chart of the stars and checked it off against a bewildering set of tables. By the time he was finished, the fire had burned down to pale ashes and the frost was decorating the inside of the window with spectacular crystalline designs.

'We have about a month,' said Barnstable. His eyes were brilliant with excitement as he held up the page which contained his final, indecipherable calculations. By contrast, Jack felt his spirit mean and sluggish and full of scepticism. He wondered, not for the first time, how someone could reach Barnstable's age and still appear as innocent as a child.

'A month for what?' he asked.

'All attempts to undertake the Great Work must begin under the rule of Aries. The most auspicious conjunction will occur on the third of April.' He grinned gleefully at Jack. 'Do you feel ready?'

Jack found that he had no answer. He could not say whether he was ready or not, since he still had no clear idea of what would be involved. He shrugged, helplessly.

The alchemist looked disappointed. 'Perhaps not,' he said. 'Never mind. There is no sense in rushing things; we'll neither of us be puffers.' He sighed deeply. 'All things being equal, it will probably be better to wait for another year.'

Jack's hesitancy was washed aside as his spirits rose on a gushing tide. 'A year!' he said. 'Oh no. No. I can't wait for another year, whatever it is I have to do. I'll be ready in a month, I'm sure I will!'

'That's all I needed to know,' said Barnstable, and Jack caught a fleeting glint of the trickster in his eyes before a radiant smile concealed it. 'It is the sure sign that the work is ready to begin.'

Chapter Twenty-six

OVER the following weeks, Jack worked harder than ever. The alchemist chose certain key documents from his library which he insisted that Jack read or re-read. And although, when he had finished them, Jack could still not claim to understand them, they were at least imprinted upon his mind. There, very gradually they began to create a new template for existence which did not depend upon the world outside but the one inside. Jack's insights were rare and incomplete, but he began to recognise the Red King as representing something within him, certain moods and characteristics. The shining lion resided within him as well, lost in the shadows, waiting to be discovered. The snake lurked in dark waters, dimly perceived, possessed of no understanding beyond its own immediate desires. The White Queen was a painful emptiness, misty and vague, her back perpetually turned towards him. And in the early hours of the morning, when Jack hunched over smoky candles and worked over the texts and drawings again and again, Hermes presided over them all with profound and mischievous wisdom.

The roof blew off the chicken house in a storm, but although Jack offered to take a day off and mend it, the alchemist wouldn't allow it. Instead, he offered the hens the use of the scullery, which they readily accepted. Meanwhile, work in the laboratory intensified. The techniques of extraction and purification that Jack had learnt now had to be put into practice as he prepared the ingredients he would actually use in his own Great Work. Barnstable would tolerate no laxity at all; everything had to be done to perfection if the undertaking was to stand any chance of success. Fires burned throughout the day as Jack refined his materials, then refined them further, and further again. At times his frustration was enormous, but the calm, unyielding presence of the alchemist acted as a constraint upon his impatience and began to forge a new meticulousness within him.

Even so, his perspective on the whole affair remained unstable. He vacillated between intense enthusiasm and bitter cynicism, to the extent that his spirits seemed attached to some gigantic pendulum which swung this way and that beyond his control. The persistent changes from inflation to dejection exhausted him; left him washed out and struggling to continue. The alchemist observed every rise and fall with intense concern, but made no effort at intervention of any kind. He remained humorous but firm, cajoling Jack onwards, containing his fluctuations of mood in his own, inviolate consistency. And, as time went on, Jack began to be aware that the preparations were creating a momentum of their own, as though the Great Work, waiting there in the future, was exerting its own attraction, pulling Jack onwards almost beyond the limits of his endurance. It both frightened and encouraged him. He had become involved in something which seemed infinitely larger than himself, and there was to be no turning back.

The auspicious day arrived much faster than Jack would have wished. He woke before dawn with a sour taste in his mouth and a black dread in his heart. He had slept fitfully and didn't feel rested at all, but no matter how hard he tried he could not retreat into the oblivion of sleep. He turned on to his back and stared into the darkness beneath the ceiling of the loft, searching for a way of escape. It occurred to him that he could just go; slip away and disappear, as he had left London and Yorkshire. But as though he heard Jack's thoughts, the alchemist stirred on the other side of the wooden partition, sighing and yawning as he always did in the mornings, then laughing and chirruping to himself like a young child as he dressed.

'Good morning, Jack,' he called through the wall.

'Good morning.'

'Remember what day it is?'

'Christmas,' said Jack, caustically.

Barnstable laughed all the way down the ladder and out into the back yard. Gritting his teeth, Jack abandoned his warm bed and got dressed.

Downstairs, he lit a candle and slumped into a chair. The alchemist came in again, buttoning his flies and shaking the dew from his boots. He perceived Jack's mood immediately.

'Not feeling terribly optimistic, then?' he said. When Jack made no reply, he continued, 'Take heart now. Take heart.'

'I don't know what it is I think I'm doing,' said Jack. 'I'm not sure what it's all about.'

Barnstable said nothing, but began clearing the ashes from the previous evening in his usual, painstaking manner.

'I never believed it,' Jack went on. 'Marley was right all along. It is a sort of madness.'

Barnstable clicked his tongue with mild impatience. 'Oh, not all that stuff about delusion again, Jack. It's very boring.' He stopped what he was doing and sat back on his heels. 'Why on earth would you have gone through all this hard work if you didn't intend to see it through?'

Jack made no answer and, after a moment or two, the alchemist said, 'I think that you do believe it. You may have forgotten for a moment, that's all, just as you forgot about the *prima materia*, even though you had it in your pocket.' He grew reflective, gazing into the empty hearth. The humour and mischief that normally animated his face departed and were replaced by a solemn reverence that Jack had never seen there before.

'Sometimes I think this art may happen despite us and not because of us,' he said softly. 'Even I do not claim to understand it in its entirety.'

The candle guttered, appeared to die, then sprang into life again. Jack shivered, knowing against all reason that they were in the presence of Hermes. Barnstable rocked on his heels for a moment, then sighed and straightened up.

'You are right in one way, though,' he said. 'You must not expect too much. For every Great Work that succeeds, a thousand fail.'

'A thousand?'

'Yes. Or more. I made my first attempts before you were born, but it was not so very long ago that I finally met with success.'

'You made gold, you mean?'

'Yes. I made gold.'

'Then why have I never seen it? Where is it?'

Outside the window, the sky was just beginning to turn from black to deep blue. The alchemist reached for kindling.

'I think you know the answer to that,' he said. 'If you don't, you will, in time. But now let's get on and have some breakfast. You have a long day ahead of you.'

When they had eaten, Barnstable went with Jack to the door of the workshop.

'I'll leave food inside the door for you from time to time,' he said. 'You need worry about nothing apart from your work, between now and the time it is finished.'

'Won't you be helping me?' said Jack.

'Of course not. You have read all you need to read and learned all you need to learn. I would only be in your way. But I shall be nearby if you should get into any trouble. And my thoughts will be with you, night and day.'

'Night and day? How long will it take, then?'

The alchemist smiled softly. 'Only you can know that, Jack. You will know, though, you need not worry. Just remember, take your time. Don't be a . . .'

'. . . puffer, I know,' Jack interrupted.

Barnstable laughed delightedly. He ruffled Jack's hair with exuberant affection, then left, closing the door behind him.

Jack stood still and looked around him. He had spent time in the workshop every day for the last six months, but the atmosphere was quite different now that he was facing an indeterminate time there alone. He found that he had no clear idea at all of what he was about to do and he began to wonder if he might not be better to wait for another year, after all. The prospect galvanized him into action. He stepped forward into the workshop and began to gather his thoughts. His own vessel, the one that had been set aside for him more than three years ago, was sitting on the marble surface of the work-table surrounded by the ingredients that he had spent the last weeks preparing for it. Beside the athanor was a good pile of sea coal and charcoal, enough to last for several weeks. Jack hoped that he would not be expected to use it all, nor all the candles which were stacked in a wooden box above it. The prospect of being alone for so long filled him with dread, and provoked in him a necessity for immediate action; anything at all to distract him from the painful thoughts and memories which lurked beneath the surface of his consciousness.

He set to work, carefully laying the makings of a fire in the outer chamber of the athanor. When it was alight, he moved over to the table and began to examine the possibilities. The open neck of his vessel, his philosopher's egg, looked up at him like an eager eye. He was impatient to start filling it, but now that the moment had come, he found himself seized by bewilderment. He had read dozens of lists and formulas in the old books, but all of them had been different. He could not remember even one of them in its entirety. Red sulphur, at least, was common to all of them. He reached for it and, as he did so, he was filled with relief. It didn't matter. Since he didn't believe that he could make gold, he could put whatever he liked into the egg. All he needed to do was to cook it for a reasonable length of time, then declare the work finished and return it to the alchemist. The ordeal would at least be over.

Whistling cheerfully, he measured out random quantities of sulphur and white lead, of arsenic and sal ammoniac and, with a little more solemnity, mercury. He had fitted the stopper and was about to begin the long process of sealing the neck when he suddenly found his hand reaching towards his waistcoat pocket. He had forgotten it again. The *prima materia*.

Slowly, carefully, Jack took it out and laid it on his palm. It looked so ordinary, just a small, dark stone, primitive among the highly refined elements on the table. His confusion returned, redoubled. The trouble was that references to the *prima materia* in the texts were always vague and elusive. Some of them suggested that the stone, ground to a fine powder, was all that should be contained within the vessel, and that the other elements would arise from it in the alchemical process. Others were more vague, giving nothing more than hints about the nature of the stone, the impurities which resided in it and the gold which would result from its incubation.

Jack found himself stuck. His knowledge of chemistry was by no means profound, but it was sufficient for him to know that a piece of common stone was unlikely to contribute to a fusion of highly refined elements in any significant way. On the contrary, it seemed likely to pollute the whole process. Yet it had to be important. If it wasn't, why had he been sent through such an ordeal to find it and fetch it back? He was on the point of going out and asking for help when the alchemist's words came back to him.

'You have read all you need to read and learned all you need to learn.'

With a sudden, profound chill, Jack knew that he was looking for the wrong kind of help. It wasn't the alchemist who was required to oversee the experiment, but someone else. Slowly he approached the curtain at the darker end of the room and drew it away from the picture beneath. Hermes looked out across the workshop and immediately the atmosphere was augmented by his presence: it was brightened and purified, as though new life had been born out of drabness and doubt.

Jack looked again at the stone in his hand. It was, once again, much more than a stone and he now had no doubt that it must go into the vessel. He reached for a mortar, the largest and strongest of them and, with a satisfying sense of conviction, he dropped the little stone into it.

But the process of reducing the *prima materia* proved more difficult than Jack had anticipated. It would not crack under pressure from the pestle, and when he tried to pound it a sharp pain shot up his arm and landed like a blow in his solar plexus. He stepped back and observed the stone, still lying intact in the bottom of the mortar. It had been with him so long it was like a part of him, and it seemed to emanate some quality of being, his own being, apart from him yet still somehow connected. To destroy it would be to destroy himself.

He looked up at Hermes on the wall. There was still no doubt about what he had to do. He took up the pestle again and began to hammer at the stone, gently at first and then with more force. It cracked, and a shudder went through him, but still he went on, pounding it into smaller and smaller pieces, every fracture like a dismantling of his own being, at his own hand. The realisation terrified him, but instead of stopping he fell into a frenzy, hammering and grinding until his arm ached and there was nothing but gritty sand in the bottom of the mortar. Then he stopped, his heart thumping, his breath ragged in his throat. With hands that shook from muscle fatigue, he tipped the contents into the neck of the vessel and replaced the stopper again. And as he began the long, painstaking process of making an impermeable seal, he knew beyond any doubt what had happened. In crushing the stone, the *prima materia*, he had crushed himself, disintegrated his being and sealed it into the womblike darkness of the egg. All that remained within him was a painful vacuum. Only time would tell whether the work of reconstitution would meet with success.

Chapter Twenty-seven

JACK settled the philosopher's egg into the inner chamber of the athanor, packing it around with fine, crumbly earth as an insulator. When he had finished, and tended to the fire and the dampers, he became infected by a strange restlessness, a certainty that there was something wrong; something he had forgotten. It was quite some time before he realised what it was. The shutters were open and the grey afternoon light was leaking in through the misty window. Neither the alchemist nor any of his books had mentioned the need for darkness, but Jack felt it. Since his correlate, the *prima materia*, was enshrined in darkness, it was only correct that he should be, as well. He closed the shutters and barred them, and hung the thick blanket that Barnstable had left for him over them, shutting out the daylight entirely. Then he settled himself on a stool beside the athanor and waited.

Time passed, but Jack had no perception of it. His mind was as empty as the darkness which surrounded him and he was aware of nothing beyond an acute anxiety which hung like a loom weight beneath his ribcage. He flattened his hands on the clay of the range beside the athanor and laid his head upon them. The clay was warm. Inside the great oven, his egg was warm as well, beginning to incubate. A pressure began to exert itself around the edges of Jack's inner darkness and he sat up, fearful of the images which were trying to invade. He reached for a candle and the tinder box, but before he had time to strike a light, the door of the workshop opened and something was placed on the floor inside it. Jack opened his mouth to call, but the door was already closed again. There was to be no reprieve, not yet.

He lit the candle and ate the supper that the alchemist had

left for him, then tended the fire in the athanor and returned to his seat beside it. The meal meant that it was evening and Jack was about to enter his first night in the workshop. He dreaded it, knowing that he could not allow himself to sleep, for fear that the fire would burn down and the work would spoil. How many nights would there be? How many could he survive? He sat vacantly until the candle burned down and died. Feeling his way in the dark, he tended the fire and then, trusting his hands to warn him of any change in the temperature, he dropped his head onto them again.

To his surprise, he could hear sound coming through them. It did not come from the athanor or he would surely have heard it before. Since there was no other source of it, it had to be coming from the vessel, the egg itself. It was a sorrowful sound; a sighing or keening; the whimpering of a lost hound or an abandoned child. As Jack listened, his attention falling towards it, it began to take form. He had heard it before.

Without warning, the memories assailed him. He was standing in the graveyard surrounded by mourners, all of them gathered like crows around a yawning hole. A priest stood at the head of the grave, droning on with words that Jack could not understand. A small coffin was being lowered into the hole. The sound he was hearing seemed to come from his own constricted throat.

Jack turned his head on his hands, but the vision remained, playing itself out relentlessly. Before it was finished it was replaced by another; a similar, but different funeral, a different coffin. One by one he watched his brothers and sisters as they were lowered into the ground but now, engulfed in lonely darkness as he was, he felt the grief of it as he had not felt it at the time. Then, it had been too much to bear. He remembered running, running through the streets, crossing his neighbourhood again and again, backwards and forwards, wearing himself down to exhaustion, falling asleep beside the fire.

His mother's haggard face appeared. 'Another one,' she said. 'Where will I find the money for the coffin?' She held an egg in her hand. It dropped.

It would be rotten, it would smash and spread its foul green corruption throughout his life. Jack gasped and sat up, staring into the darkness, wiping the terrifying impression from his mind. His hands were full of pins and needles, but beneath them the clay was still warm. He shook the blood back into them and groped numbly for the flint and a pinch of tinder. Shadows reared behind the clean, young light of the new candle. He lit a second one, and a third, his hands shaking as he sought to banish the darkness. From the end wall, Hermes stared out at him, hovering on his winged heels, cold and indifferent.

Jack was amazed to discover, by the state of the fire, how long he had been lost in dreams. Had it been allowed to go untended for much longer it would have gone out, and it took Jack a good deal of the skills the alchemist had taught him to coax it back into health. He succeeded, though, and he was confident enough in the athanor's insulating properties to know that the work would not have suffered. When he put an ear to it again, it was still singing, though with a different voice this time. It was higher than before, like a wind that sighed around a house at night, rising and falling, carrying him with it into a bare landscape where the Red King, Jack himself, wandered with a pale mist at his side that should have been the White Queen. Above him, in some indeterminate place on a hill or in the sky, Hermes was loitering, up to no good as usual. The rotten egg that had haunted Jack's entire life was in his hand. Otherwise there was nothing but the song, soft and persistent and unutterably lonely.

How long he remained there, Jack could not tell, but when he next raised his head and lighted new candles, his breakfast was waiting inside the door and it was quite cold. He ate it in the same way that he tended the fire, dutifully, without enthusiasm. Afterwards it sat like a stone in his innards, as though the despair which gripped him resented anything which served the purpose of keeping him alive. He paced restlessly for a while and visited the tiny latrine in the corner of the room, but there was no escaping from the work. Soon he was back on his stool again, his head on his hands, listening to the sound of the vessel in the athanor.

Throughout the days and nights which followed, it sang its alchemical songs of fermentations and putrifactions, of separations and conjunctions, and Jack lived through them all. He dreamed of his father in Davy Jones' Locker, and in Portsmouth, feeding a new family like cuckoos in a stolen nest. He saw his mother die again and again, watched the final coffin enter the cold earth while another priest murmured over it. He was taken in by Tom and beaten by him, over and over again. He found the beautiful Arab colt and loved him and lost him.

And then there was Eleanor. Jack had loved her, but she hadn't given him a chance. He had meant nothing to her, as if he really had been a frog. He found that he could forgive everyone for what they had done to him, even Tom, even the Duke. But when he thought of Eleanor he felt nothing but humiliation. His soul was filled with bitterness as he remembered how hard he had tried to become what she wanted, and how she had rejected him despite everything. How could he ever forgive her for what she had done?

Jack endured as he imagined the contents of the vessel to be enduring, trapped as he was in the warm darkness. Sleep and waking merged into one another, and he lost track of the number of bowls which appeared inside the door and were taken away again. Like a tapped spring, the painful memories ran through his mind, hour after hour. He shed no tears, as though they were denied exit by the hermetic seal of his endurance, but he felt every loss all the more acutely because of it. He moved through the darkness in slow misery, emptying ashes, groping among the dusty coals, blowing on dim embers with breath as faint as his heart. He feared for the work, for himself, for the lonely Red King fading away into mist like his White Queen.

Then the voice of the sacred vessel changed again. Its tone lowered in pitch and seemed to Jack to be filled with menace. In his bleak inner landscape, Hermes lifted his hand. The egg was poised to fall. Jack braced himself.

Hermes opened his hand. It was all over. But in the strange, suspended instants that followed, Jack became aware of another presence. He looked around. He was not alone. Eleanor was there. Not the White Queen. Eleanor. Jack understood now that he had made her into something that she never was and could never be. She was just herself, a young woman, tall and confident, doing her best to make her own way in a world full of contradictions and obstacles, just as he was. Like him, she had made choices in life, and she had found the courage to stick to them, despite the odds. And if her choices didn't correspond with his, was she to be blamed? The moment of illumination was still with him. The egg, somehow, was still falling. There was still time. Time to realise that Eleanor was not to blame for his feelings. She could not have acted other than she did. The only things that were to blame for his disappointment were his own desires and expectations.

The alchemist spoke, or was it Hermes?

'Tell me about delusion.'

That was where the delusion lay. He could do nothing about those early years; his birth and his upbringing were beyond his powers to influence. But his subsequent choices had been his own responsibility. Wealth had not brought him happiness. Marrying Eleanor would not have brought him happiness, either. He would have found new things to desire, even to need. The alchemist knew that. Nell had known it as well. But Jack had needed this time; this long, painful darkness, to come to the realisation himself.

His anger and hurt melted away. The Red King and the White Queen were as much a part of his inner world as the red sulphur and white lead were a part of the alchemy happening inside the sealed vessel. They could never exist in the real world outside, where people were people with all their idiosyncrasies and imperfections. Only in here, in his mind, could a total union between them exist. And in the vessel, perhaps. Red sulphur and white lead.

He reached out and took Eleanor into his arms. As they embraced he felt himself becoming complete.

The egg was still falling, still in timeless suspension. Jack watched it, seeing in it the relic that he had found floating in the Thames and that he had never dared to open. It was Barnstable's egg, and his own egg as well; the one which was still cooking inside the athanor. He could stop it, he knew. He could stop the work and he could step out of the workshop and return to his old way of being. But he was ready now. Ready to know.

The egg, released from his doubt, fell to the ground and smashed. Pure, molten gold spilled out, immersing them both, dissolving them into its bright substance. Jack felt himself becoming part of the golden fluid, and for an indeterminate amount of time he floated in a weightless state; a blissful freedom from the constriction of beliefs and desires. He had let them all go, and a new life free of striving and suffering awaited him as soon as he was ready to step into it.

He stretched out his arms and stood up. He couldn't see himself, but he knew how he looked. He was a child again; himself reborn. On his head was a helmet with wings. In his hand, he held a staff, and around it a snake was entwined.

Chapter Twenty-eight

THE silence was total. Jack sat up, rubbing his eyes, and felt around him on the workbench for a candle.

The light hurt his eyes. He squinted and blinked and, as his vision cleared, the first thing he saw was two bowls sitting beside the door, both of them full. He could not remember either of them arriving.

Beside his knee the athanor was stone cold. Inside it, the vessel was silent. It was all over.

And yet, just beginning. Jack strode over to the window and pulled down the thick blanket. He unbarred the shutters and pulled them aside, then opened the window itself. A heavy rain was falling, but he had never seen a more beautiful day. The river was in full spate, rolling and churning along on its way to the sea. Jack put his head out of the window and laughed as the rain soaked into his hair, running into his collar and down his back like cold little mice. He stayed there for long minutes, delighting in the freshness, until the sound of the door handle turning caught his attention.

The alchemist stepped inside the workshop and leant against the door, crossing his arms and his feet. He said nothing, but raised his eyebrows questioningly.

Jack grinned and nodded. 'It's finished.'

'Let's have a look, then.' Barnstable unfolded himself and moved across to the athanor. Together, he and Jack raised the heavy lid and looked inside. The vessel was still buried in the earth, which had been baked to a fine, grey powder. Jack uncovered it delicately and lifted it out. It was still intact and still, to Jack's surprise, slightly warm. He set it down gently on top of the workbench.

'Dissolve the body and coagulate the spirit,' he said.

The alchemist nodded, observing Jack closely, the familiar, impish smile on his face. Jack returned it like a mirror and together they burst into delighted laughter.

'Well,' said Barnstable eventually, gesturing towards the vessel with his thumb. 'What's inside it?'

'Gold,' said Jack.

'Shall we have a look and see?'

'We could,' said Jack. He picked up the vessel and weighed it in his hand. It glowed with a mysterious vibrancy and for a long time Jack observed it, absorbed in its ancient secrecy. Then he said, 'Or perhaps I will do what you did with yours when you made it.'

'And what was that?' said the alchemist. He was watching with amused expectancy.

Jack raised the vessel like a toast towards the picture on the wall then turned and, with perfect aim, flung it out through the window and into the rushing water of the Thames. As he faced the alchemist again, there was a mischievous glint in his eye.

'Offer it to Hermes,' he said.

Barnstable beamed with delight, and together the two alchemists set about tidying the workshop. On the river, Jack's finished work ducked and bobbed on the current, already well on its way towards the hungry streets of London town.

THE END